This book is very exciting. There is definitely a lot of drama that can be related to. I couldn't put the book down. I was always wondering what was going to happen next. Next. – LaTasha Martin, Boston, MA

Very catching and very entertaining. I couldn't stop reading the book. Good to the end. - Alphonso Gwinn, Hyde Park, MA

I Stumbled But I Didn't Fall

CHERYL BONITA MARTIN

authorHOUSE®

AuthorHouse™
1663 Liberty Drive
Bloomington, IN 47403
www.authorhouse.com
Phone: 1-800-839-8640

First published by AuthorHouse 10/19/2010

ISBN: 978-1-4520-4140-7 (e)
ISBN: 978-1-4520-4139-1 (sc)
ISBN: 978-1-4520-4141-4 (hc)

Library of Congress Control Number: 2010909505

Printed in the United States of America

This book is printed on acid-free paper.

Foreward

This book is for all women (and men who can relate). The book takes you on a journey of experiencing the joys and the pains of relationships, overcoming obstacles and finding the strength of finding yourself. I would like to share this story with anyone who may have had similar experiences.

In loving memory of my grandmother Victoria Martin.
Rest in Peace.

Dedication

I would like to dedicate this book to my mom Ella M. Martin, my daughter Sheneé Martin, my granddaughter Asia Martin, my sister LaTasha Martin, my niece Jaélah Martin and my brother Reginald Martin.

Special Thanks

A special thanks goes out to my cousin Charles S. Martin of Wake Forest, NC for his support.

Lee Martin of Roslindale, MA. Thank you for coming through for us financially when we were in need.

Alphonso Gwinn of Hyde Park, MA. Thank you for being a good friend to me and taking the time to read my manuscript.

Chapter 1

My mom worked long hours and traveled a lot with her job to support my brother and I. Our neighbor, Ms. Granny who is a mother figure to all of the mothers in the neighborhood, had come to realize that my brother and I were always home alone. My mom was a single parent. Therefore, Ms. Granny thought it would be a good idea that we live with her for a while so that my mom can work and make her money. My mom agreed. So we were adopted, not legally, into Ms. Granny's home. I was six years old and my brother Nate was two years old. We were too young to know what a family was supposed to mean, nevertheless represent. Overall, my life as a young girl growing up with this fake adopted family was complicated, confusing and miserable as hell. I was a shy girl but very loving. I was smart and I was wise. Always curious. I could be opinionated too. Ms. Granny did all she could do to support us with the help of my mom's money she sent to Ms. Granny on a monthly basis. This included helping Ms. Granny's deadbeat husband, who was a drunk and a dope head. I remember when I was in elementary school, I went to the principal's office and told the principal that Mr. Scott had beaten Ms. Granny, punched her in the nose and knocked her to the ground. I was so afraid to go back to Ms. Granny's house afterwards. Mr. Scott always did what he wanted to do and it didn't make one damn difference what any of us had to say. It was plain and simply out of the question.

I used to hope and pray that Ms. Granny would leave her husband or my mom would come for us or Ms. Granny's husband would die or something. She would put him out, only to be back in a matter of a week or two. I was very nervous. I was so nervous that I used to pull out the hair on the sides of my head. Front and back. Just craziness over being nervous around this dumb fool.

My brother Nate and I had a lot of fear of Mr. Scott when we were growing up. Mr. Scott would make us eat all of our food, even if we were full. We just did not get him at all. What was his mental problems or issues? I never really understood why he was so mean to us. Was it because Ms. Granny took us in? What did he care? It wasn't like he was shelling out any of his money to take care of us. He never helped Ms. Granny in any kind of way. In fact, he used to gamble heavily, never had any money, had other women and mistreated Ms. Granny without any respect whatsoever.

There was a lot of mental and physical abuse Mr. Scott caused on Ms. Granny. It affected me and my brother as well. He used to beat us like we were his kids, punch us in the head and fight us like we were a grown man his own size or one of the homies that did him wrong. And to top it off, he never had any remorse of what he did. It was beyond us and very nerve racking. Ms. Granny had no say. It was sad. It was like we deserved this kind of abuse, just because Ms. Granny took us in. Mr. Scott had children of his own, but they disowned him. I'm not surprised and I can definitely see why. My brother and I would talk amongst ourselves and put both of our hands up in the air and look at one another and be like "what the fuck is this dude's problem?" He is not wrapped too tight. Mentally, we were abused and confused. We were kids for crying out loud. "Why would you mistreat children?" I remember when Nate and I would have to whisper to Ms. Granny for something to eat or to get some water. Mr. Scott would come in there with his loud talking voice asking, "what yall need?" Ask me, not Ms. Granny. I'm the head of this god damn household. I rolled my eyes in my head. Ms. Granny had no control at all, nevermind us. After all, we were just there temporarily. It was amazing and mind blowing. I really believe Ms. Granny is afraid of Mr. Scott. He is a very dominant, mean ass looking man! Noone liked him at all. I always felt that it was going to be me or my brother that killed him, unless he kills us first.

I never really could understand how a human being could be so self-ish towards his own wife. Mr. Scott seemed to be the type of individual who wanted everything to himself. He didn't care. There were many times that I can remember while staying at Ms. Granny's house, she would be low on heat and could not afford to get heat in the house. Ms. Granny would ask Mr. Scott for money so she could get the tank filled with oil and he would never have it. That or he didn't want to give it to her. There was always an argument about money. Ugh! "How could Ms. Granny be with someone like this, I would ask myself?" She is so nice and so kind. But, being the kind and generous woman she is, Ms. Granny would go to the bank and clean out her savings just to get oil in the house to keep everyone warm. Mind you, we weren't even her kids! We needed hot water to wash our ass, including Mr. Scott washing his big, nasty stinking ass. This left Ms. Granny broke without any money in the bank and to top it off, she had to take her whole social security check, along with the money my mom sent monthly to help pay her bills, our afterschool care, buy food and clothing, while Mr. Scott sat back, ate, stayed warm and enjoyed his retirement check all to himself without a care in the fucking world.

He never felt guilty about any of this at all. Imagine that? That's what the fuck we couldn't comprehend. Most people that have a conscience would feel some type of shame or remorse. But no, not Mr. "fucked up" Scott. We could not stand him and he definitely could not stand us, including Ms. Scott. It did not phase him one bit either. In fact, he hated us – all of us! That goes to show you how selfish, immature and uncaring he was. In some ways, he was like a big brother to us and Ms. Granny's oldest son. He didn't even care about Ms. Granny or maybe never really even loved her. It was all about his convenience. Mr. Scott acts as though he was some kind of king or something. He ate out of his mouth and shitted out of his ass the same way we did. Believe me, his shit stunk big time too. He sheds blood just like we do and he is going to die just like we are. He has no idea what he put all of us through. No idea whatsoever.

About three months down the line, I went to Ms. Granny with some hurtful news about her bitch ass husband. I was straight up, straight out and to the point with it. I didn't gave a damn at this point. "Ms. Granny, I have something to tell you." What's that, sweetie? I sighed. I asked her not to tell Mr. Scott because I was in such great fear that I thought he would wound up hurting me. I said "Mr. Scott has been messing around with Ms. Johnson sexually and Ms. Johnson's thirteen year old daughter, Marissa." She looked at me in total shock. I saw Mr. Scott touch Marissa's breast with my own eyes and then he pulled out his dick and showed it to her. He even asked Marissa to kiss it. I was peeping from Marissa's bedroom. Are you sure, Denise? Yes, I am sure, Ms. Granny. I'm sorry this hurts you Ms. Granny, but you need to know and I couldn't keep it in me any longer. I remember over hearing Ms. Granny confronting Mr. Scott with this and he tried to lie about it. No, actually he LIED about it! I really didn't know if Ms. Granny believed me or not, or maybe she did. All in all, she still stayed with her fucked up husband and I just could not figure that out for the life of me. What was her problem or what was her thinking process? Life went on as usual.

Mr. Scott also had major control over me and my brother's life. He made all of the decisions whether we liked it or not. One time my brother said he was going to call our father to let him know what was going on. Mr. Scott would not let him do so. Ms. Granny disagreed with Mr. Scott on this. But as usual, Ms. Granny had no control over Mr. Scott's decision. Well guess what, Mr. Scott wasn't having it. There was even an incident when my brother got into a little trouble with the law and Ms. Granny called our mom to come down for support. When Ms. Granny asked Mr. Scott to come along for support, he responded by saying "he ain't going to no damn court behind no nappy headed little boy that wasn't his or hers for that matter." That was so sad. He controlled everything, punk ass motherfucker. That's exactly what he was. We couldn't stand him. We often wished he would drop and die. Please Jesus, take him out of here! Poof, be gone!

Once I had a boyfriend named Johnnie. And for some reason, Mr. Scott never cared for Johnnie. But that was his problem, not mine. Who the hell did Mr. Scott think he was? Who died and made him God? Johnnie and his friend came over to visit with me one day. He ranged the bell once or twice. Mr. Scott came downstairs and said to Johnnie "Man, you don't have to ring the bell all crazy like that" and Johnnie said "I only rung the bell it once, man." To make a long story short, an argument broke out. Mr. Scott punched Johnny in the nose, pulled out a knife and stabbed him on his arm. Johnnie's friend tried to get between the two of them to break it up. In the interim, Johnnie's friend ended up getting stabbed in the leg and his friend ended up stabbing Mr. Scott in self defense. I was so afraid that I ran upstairs crying and screaming for Ms. Granny. Shortly after I got upstairs, Mr. Scott came

5

to the door of the back room where I was. He asked me to open the door but I wouldn't, so he went and got a tooth pick or something and stuck it through the small hole on the door knob. The door opened. Mr. Scott grabbed me, threw me to the ground, punched me in the lip and started stomping the shit out of me. All I remember is that I broke loose, ran passed Ms. Granny and ran to the hospital. I could hear Ms. Granny yelling and carrying on as I ran passed her. I got treated for my busted lip and they took x-rays of my head to make sure I wasn't having any head injuries or internal bleeding. I found out that Johnnie's friend was at the hospital being treated for his stab wound in the leg. Mr. Scott was later admitted. I had hoped he died.

Mr. Scott later apologized to me and told me that Johnnie didn't stab him, that it was his friend and that he was going to press charges against him. But when Mr. Scott couldn't find Johnnie's friend, he turned the tables and told the police that Johnnie stabbed him. I told Mr. Scott I was not going to lie for him if it went to court. In court, I told the judge how Mr. Scott said in the beginning that Johnnie wasn't responsible and that I better tell the court that Johnnie was. He also threatened me by saying that if he EVER saw me with Johnnie again, he will light my ass up. Ms. Granny was caught in the middle between me and her punk ass husband. I couldn't understand where Mr. Scott's head was. I'm telling you, this nigger was nutty, a fruit cake! When Ms. Granny's daugher-in-law passed away, my friend Linda had to ride with Mr. Scott because me and my brother rode in the limo with the rest of Ms. Granny's family. Funny how Mr. Scott didn't ride with the family. What does that tell you? Ha!

I couldn't understand Linda's behavior after everything was over. When everyone was at Ms. Granny's house for dinner, Linda pulled me aside and we went downstairs.

"I need to talk to you Denise." About what, I asked? I have something to tell you about Mr. Scott. What about him? Don't say anything to Ms. Granny, but on our way to the funeral home, Mr. Scott came on to me. He asked me if he gives me his number, would I call him and come over his house when no one is there. As old as he is, I asked? Please. I went totally off, Denise. Mr. Scott was like, "Linda, I don't want to stick it in, I just want to lick it." Dumb ass motherfucker, I said in anger! I told Mr. Scott that I am going to tell Ms. Granny. "Do you know what that asshole had the nerve to say to me?" "No, what," I asked? Mr. Scott was like "can't you keep a damn secret Linda?" "I told that ignorant fucker to go screw himself." "Old nasty bastard." Girl, I thought I was going to vomit. I know you did.

How could you all put up with him? He's a sick person. Mr. Scott has a serious problem. I couldn't tell Ms. Granny. I felt more comfortable coming to you. I understand Linda.

Linda and I went back in the house. Mr. Scott was sitting around the table eating, talking and laughing with everyone like everything was on the up and up with the family. Does he have a conscience? Does he care about anything or anyone? Nope.

Mr. Scott is also a big liar. I told Ms. Granny about my conversation with Linda. She confronted Mr. Scott and naturally he lied. Again. I love Ms. Granny, but I don't get her. Why can't she leave his stupid ass.

I called my mother and told her that it was time for her to come back home and get a place for the three of us. We needed to get out of Ms. Granny's house before someone gets hurt or gets killed. My patience is weighing me down. I told my mom all that has happened. I told her that Mr. Scott has a problem deep within himself. He manipulates people, he's selfish and he has no conscience whatsoever. My mom agreed to start looking for a job and to come back home.

Finally, Ms. Granny did not trust Mr. Scott any longer nor believed anything that came out of his nasty mouth. Thank God. He's gone behind her back and pulled all kinds of stunts. Nevertheless, Granny still did not leave Mr. Scott. That's beyond me. But I still love her. I will continue to pray for Ms. Granny.

I realized the years we have been with Ms. Granny, she has worked very hard to support herself along with me and my brother to make ends meet, and all along she has been used and taken advantage of by her no good husband, Mr. Scott.

If Jesus can forgive, I can forgive. I still have a lot of resentment towards Mr. Scott. What an experience to see with a man and a woman at such a young age. I can see right through him. I just hope this doesn't affect how I view men in my relationships to come. I have always been told that I was one of the most beautiful people around, because there are a lot of people who would find it very hard to forgive a person so easily. I really can't relate to him and I don't have too much of a conversation for Mr. Scott, except for a general conversation that I would have with anyone that I'm not too comfortable with.

Far and foremost, God has seen me and my brother through this ordeal and did not allow any harm come to us by Mr. Scott.

This portion of our childhood has been a mental and emotional roller coaster ride caused by Mr. Scott. I believe behind this kind of abuse Mr. Scott imposed upon my brother Nate, Nate found his comfort zone in the streets and through drugs.

I always remembered, "what goes around, will surely come around, every DOG has his day and when that day comes around, Mr. Scott's cookie is not only going to fall, it's going to crumble." Karma is a bitch!

Chapter 2
_____

My brother and I were very close growing up. We definitely would fight each other. I would sometimes kick my brother's ass and he would tell my mother. Of course, I got into trouble. My brother and I were pretty good kids. Mom always got us basically everything we needed and wanted. Nate had football games and I danced in talent shows at the community school. Back in the day, there were a lot of kids in the neighborhood. My uncle and aunt owned the three family house we lived in with our mother and stepfather. Although, we had a pretty decent childhood in a working class neighborhood, there was something missing from my brother's life: a father figure. I believe this all stems from living in the past with Ms. Granny and her crazy ass husband, Mr. Scott. My brother had no man to look up to as a father nor had he had a man to call him son. Although we had a stepfather, he didn't do his job as a father and he never took time with my brother to show him things about how a young man should be. My mother used to ask Calvin if he would take Nate with him sometimes when he goes fishing, but Calvin never had the time. It was like Calvin resented my brother and didn't like him. For some strange reason, it was like Nate was overlooked where this man was concerned. Naturally, my brother didn't feel loved by this man. Sometimes he would even doubt my mother's love because she stayed with her husband and allowed all of this to take place. It was like she didn't have any say in the matter at all. She just sat back and let Calvin control everything; even her own kids she brought into this world. It was definitely a flashback of how Ms. Granny's husband, Mr. Scott was.

When my brother got to high school, that's when all of his troubles began. He started hanging out with his friends that were up to no good and hanging out with an older man name Rick. My mother used to tell Nate about hanging with Rick. What does an older man have in common with a fifteen year old? One thing led to another. My brother and his no good friends started slinging that dope and using drugs. Nate started out with smoking weed. Nate started skipping school, started stealing, losing weight and his attitude definitely changed dramatically. In a sense, Calvin seemed like he didn't give a fuck that Nate was caught up in this lifestyle. Just happy and hoping he falls. But then again, he never cared for my brother or never did a thing for him to help guide him in the right direction. Calvin told my mother that Nate had to leave the house and that he could never come back. There were times when my brother would call my mother to ask her if he could come by to get something to eat and to tell her that he needed a place to sleep because it was cold outside. But my mother followed her husband's stupid ass crazy rules and couldn't do a damn thing for my brother. If Calvin was around, my mother and I would whisper and talk about Nate. Calvin used to always ask us "how come every time I come into the kitchen, you all stop talking?" He was never interested in anything that had to do with my brother, so why should we include him? I remember once it was a cold and wintery night. My mother wanted to let my brother in the house for food and shelter, but she couldn't because of Calvin's simple ass. The only thing that my mother could do was pass Nate food through the door, which led to the cold hallway. Nate had to sleep in the hallway that night as well. Imagine what that would do to a person mentally? It would fuck you up in the head. To know that your own son can't come in your house and there is a blizzard going on outside and he has to sleep in the hallway? That wasn't cool at all. I would have left that man right then and there. No questions asked. Instead of Calvin being supportive and understanding, he was cold, uncaring and selfish. He just didn't give a fuck. Makes me sick. This felt like flashbacks all over again. In fact it was flashbacks.

As years and time when on, my brother started getting high with the heavier stuff. Crack, cocaine. He started hitting that pipe and free-basing. My mother and I always told my brother to get into a drug treatment program to help his problem. Nate tried. But like he said, it's a disease that is hard to kick. Once an addict, always an addict, he added. Even when an addict goes into recovery, he is considered a recovering addict. An addict is an addict. Bottom line. Just when we thought Nate got it together, he would let us down again. I saw that this was bringing my mother down and through a lot of pain and agony. She had problems with my brother, let alone the problems with her stupid ass husband Calvin. My mother was really depressed for a long, long, time. It used to hurt me and I used to pray to God that Nate would at least get himself together for my mother's sake. But nevertheless, the drugs over powered him and took over his life. Nate had no control over this drug war.

Another time, seems like the hundredth time, Nate decided to get help and the necessary treatment for his drug addiction to crack cocaine. He went to a program for a whole year. In that year's time, Nate had gained all his weight back, got his skin color back, talked positive, had a decent job and most importantly, had kicked the habit.

He met two recovering addicts from the program. A guy name Darryl and a guy name Jerome. They became really good friends and they all had graduated from the drug rehab program. All were on their way to a new drug free start. One thing that Darryl and Jerome didn't like was that Nate was going to move in with Lori, who is white, a recovering alcoholic and was there for him throughout the rough times. They felt that Nate didn't need to hook up with anyone at that time because he needed to be able to continue to get himself together. "Sure you two can be friends," they told Nate. But this was no time for Nate to be getting into a serious relationship with someone who already had a ready made family and to top it off, a recovering alcoholic." She had her own set of issues with substance abuse and problems. That was a stressful situation as is and they felt if Nate had a lot of stress and pressure too soon, he would relapse. "Who you telling?"

Nate decided to move in with Lori anyway. At first, it was ok. He worked, helped out with her kids, paid some of the bills and gave Lori his money to manage. That did not last too long. The next thing we knew, Nate started using again. He sold Lori's son Eric's nintendo set, clothes, etc., all for a quick hit. Lori put him out. My mother and I, especially me, started playing hardball with Nate. We told him he could not stay with us at all and that he would just have to live like a bum on the street, hoping this would wake him up. Guess what, it didn't! Lori took him back. Dumb bitch.

The next thing we heard, Lori was pregnant. Oh no. Is she really nuts? Nate put her through mad changes. He still continued to use constantly and heavily. By Lori being pregnant did not make one damn difference to Nate. The drugs were Nate's first love, not the baby-to-be. Lori used to call me or I would call her and she would be very upset and be crying and carrying on. The baby was born in June. It was a baby boy and they named him Nate, Jr. We thought by Nate having a child, it would help him realize his responsibilities as a father, considering that he grew up without one, although our stepfather Calvin was in the household. It didn't mean a thing to him. Drugs were Nate's baby, his love child.

Things didn't change or get any better with Nate and Lori. Lori would let Nate use her car and the next thing you know, Nate tells her that the car was stolen. Bullshit, I told Lori! The nigger sold your car. Nate must have sold about three cars of Lori's. I used to ask her, "why do you let him take your car knowing that he will sell it?" All Lori would say is "I don't know, I think I'm the stupid one." "Isn't that the truth," I would say. The next thing was the money. When Nate would get paid from his job he suddenly had all kinds of excuses as to why he doesn't have any money. Silly excuses at that. For instance, Nate would tell Lori payroll messed up his check and his money was short, then he would say they did not pay him and to top it off, Nate would say things like, "oh, I went to cash my check and these dudes jumped me and took all of my money." All being bullshit lies and Lori would go for it until one day a bell must have gone off in her head. Lori was fed up and done with the bullshit. Lori told Nate he had to go. She put Nate out for good. Enough was enough, she told me. Nate then got into another program. I think Nate used programs as a shelter, rather than a place to get help for his drug addiction. I told him that he is in denial and the first thing he needs to do is to get honest with himself. Nate decided to take my advice.

Nate lasted only about three weeks in the program. He claimed that the counselor was giving him a hard time because he is black, then she kicked him out. Nate also lost his good job. That was game just to get out of the program to go get high. I know all of the the tricks and all of the games. The next thing we heard, Nate moved in with a woman name Holly. Holly was cool. But she was a recovering addict herself and supposively into church at this time in her life. The difference between Holly and Lori is that Holly wasn't having the bullshit nor was she going to put up with the bullshit from Nate. Holly had been into the world of drugs and prostitution at one time, and she had been clean for about five years. I told Nate that it was going to be different with Holly. Black women won't put up with your shit like Lori did. Whatever Holly tell you to do, you better do it, because she would put your ass out in the cold in a heartbeat and won't even think twice about it. Holly told me one time, "if Nate ever sells anything in my house or steals anything from my kids, he's gone." And you better believe she wasn't bullshitting around. When Nate sold her son's jacket and sneakers, he was gone. Out of there! Once again, Nate was back in the streets, back in another program. That is just so sad.

After years of battling drug addition, arrests, being convicted of several felonies and serving time in jail, Nate is really trying to get back on his feet for once. He sounds more positive and ready to do the right things in life. For Mother's Day weekend, we had his son, Nate, Jr. and brought him to see Big Nate at the drug rehab. My brother's eyes filled up with tears. I wanted to reach out to him, but I couldn't because this is the kind of thing he needs to get out on his own and in his own time, without anyone coming to his rescue.

I saw this game way too many times to fall back into that trap. My mother and I prayed for my brother for his recovery from the drug addiction and to the dangerous and cruel world of drugs.

Let the drama begin with the men in my life.

Chapter 3

I met Michael back in the mid eighties while we were both working at the bank. I was an executive assistant in the mortgage department and he was a supervisor at one of the local branches. I was introduced to Michael by a guy name George, who was a loan officer.

I knew from the moment I met Michael, he was interested in me. He seemed to be a down-to-earth brother. Clean cut. Sharp! I was immediately attracted to him and I could tell I already liked him and would like to get to know him in time. My homegirl Carmen was like, "Denise look, he's checking you out big time." I said to her, "Please Carmen, that guy probably has a big house, a wife and some kids." So, what that mean? You are so crazy Carmen.

The next day at work, I got a phone call from Michael. I didn't recognize his voice of course. Hi, Denise, Michael said. May I ask who this is, I responded. Michael. "Michael who," I asked? "Do you remember yesterday George introduced me to you?" Oh yeah. "How are you," I asked? Good. I was just calling to say hi and to ask how your day is going. Well thanks. Hey, I was thinking, would you like to get together and go to a movie? I thought about it for a moment and decided, why not. That sounds cool. Ok, let's set up a date then. I invited Carmen to come along. You never know. You can't be too trusting these days.

The following week me, Michael and my friend Carmen went to see The Color Purple. After the movies, Carmen went her separate way and Michael walked me to my car and I told him I'll call him when I get home. There was a time Michael came to visit me and I went to visit him. I said to myself, "he's cool." I didn't have any girlfriend, boyfriend feelings for him as of yet because I was still in the checking out phase.

Michael lived in a small town, which is located on the east shore with a roommate. I would go over to Michael's once a week, usually on a Thursday or Friday evening. Sometimes he would come over to my house. One evening I invited Michael over to my house. I had mentioned to Michael that the bells were not working, so when someone comes in the door, just come on up to my place which was on the 7th floor. Around 7:00 p.m., I got a knock on my door. And without me asking who it was and assuming it was Michael, I just opened the door. When I did, guess who it was? My crazy ass friend Wayne who I use to see off and on and his friend Rob. Wayne is a guy who is a liar, a player who is trying to play the pimp role, but never succeeded and plays a lot of head games. He is also one of those superfly niggers. He had a brand new Mustang 5.0 with the T-top, he wore gold rings and chains and he was sharp as a motherfucker. Wayne wore the latest in fashion – Louis Vuitton, Gucci, leather sweat suits, and so on. You name it, he had it. Not to mention all the women he had. He was just plain and simply "A NO GOOD NIGGER." The funny thing about it is that all of the women knew how Wayne's personality and traits were and still wanted to be with him. I almost fell into that trap, but I slapped myself out of it. No thank you. I'll spare myself the headaches and the heartaches. LMAO! When I opened the door, "I asked Wayne what did he want and told him that I am expecting company any minute now?" You know he had the nerve to ask me who and is it a male or a female? I frowned and looked at him like he was nuts or something. I told him a male, as if I was supposed to lie. The minute I mentioned a male, Wayne and his friend Rob refused to leave. Suddenly, I got a knock on my door. It was Michael. I said to myself, damn it, I hope Wayne don't start no shit! For crying out loud, I wasn't even his woman. I opened the door and let Michael in. I introduced all of them. Michael could feel that there was tension in the air, so he felt it was best that he leave. I explained to Michael that he didn't have to leave, but he insisted. Ugh, I just blew any possible possibilities with Michael. I tried convincing Michael to stay, but he did not want to. Then again with Wayne's ghetto and street mentality, I figured it was best if Michael actually leaves. I did not want to be responsible for anything bad that could have possibly happened between Michael and Wayne. Wayne is crazy and trigger happy. I walked Michael to the elevator and before I knew it, Wayne comes storming out of the door acting like a wild beast, walking fast, yelling and all. He was crazy looking too. A fruit cake for sure! Wayne kept walking towards me and yelling my name out loud. Stupid. I ignored him. I kept walking with Michael towards the elevator. The elevator door opened and Michael got on and left. After the elevator doors closed, Wayne was like, "so what's up?" "I'm like," with what? "That nigger," that's what? Wayne please, save it. That's a friend of mine. What's the problem? We have no connection with one another. And besides, you don't just be popping up at my apartment with your friend out of the blue. Respect me and call me before you come popping up over here. What are you doing here anyway? Wayne started an argument. I told him that I wasn't his lady and that he and Rob would have to leave. Wayne cussed me out and said that I was through in his book. Good because he has been through in my book a long time ago. I tell you, I have the craziest experiences with men.

The next day, I got a call from Michael. He was going off. My head was spinning. First it was Wayne going off now Michael. Michael asked me, "why I played him like a fool?" I was confused and I was shocked. I tried to explained to Michael and asked him if he could hear me out, but he wouldn't. He just hung up the phone. I knew this was a done deal for Michael and me. Like most women, I got on the phone and called all my home girls and told them what happened. They all started tripping, carrying on and adding their opinions. Women can be so dramatic at times. Too funny. Oh well, "it ain't nothing but a thang." Moving right along.

Chapter 4

Two days later, my doorbell rings. Hello, I answered. It's Michael. I buzzed him up. He came in and asked, what's up? Nothing much; just reading a magazine that's about it, I responded. Why are you here Michael? Oh, I just wanted to see you, that's all. I asked Michael how everything was going with him these days? Fine, just a lot of working. Michael said that he was just dropping by to see how I was doing and that he wanted to apologize for leaving the other night and to apologize for his being disrespectful and hanging up in my face. I accepted his apology and told him not to worry about it. "Can we start over from the start," Michael asked? Sure, why not. For a moment, Michael was eyeing me up and down. I frowned and asked him what hell he was looking at. I can be so hard sometimes on a brother. He gave me that look and I said to him, do not get any ideas my friend because you are not sleeping with me if that's what you are thinking. Michael came closer to me and kissed my neck. I pulled away but Michael pulled me back towards him. "Will you please let go of me Michael?" We started messing around and one thing led to another. "I can't believe this shit." "You came over here to see how I'm doing and the next minute we

19

are engaged into something totally different." "What's the matter with you Michael," I asked? "You are crazy, that's all," I said. "Denise, I have had a thing for you since day one and the way we talk to each other on the phone and eye each other, I know you are sexually attractive to me as well." "So stop playing," Michael said. He had a point there and I was curious, but not that damn curious. It was just too soon. Leave it up to my friend Carmen, no time is too soon. "It all depends on the two individuals and the two of you are grown adults is what she would say." I am more conservative than Carmen. "You know what," I said to Michael. "After tonight, I don't think I want to see you or talk to you anymore." "Now please leave." Go! What you talking about woman? Naw, I am not down for this and although I enjoyed the moment, I can't do this. I'm sorry. I just want you to go. We can be friends but nothing more. I hope there are no hard feelings between us. So, you used me Denise? Used you? What, how? You came over here and forced yourself on me? I think you are a playgirl. Think what you want. The last time I was over here, your friend popped up and you did not make him leave. I know you are not tripping over that? Please, that is old news Michael. Get over it! Yeah, whatever Denise. Suit yourself. Michael went into the bathroom, put his pants on and left. He was pissed at me and did not even say goodbye. Does Michael realize that I could claim this as rape if I decided to be an asshole about this? This nigger is tripping just like the other one. I thought he was over what had gone down a few days ago with Wayne. I guess it still bothered him. I don't have time for all of that. My mind is made up. He came over, things happened and now I am moving on from it. I was through wasting my time with Michael. I could see the drama coming.

I called Carmen and told her the whole story. He did what, Carmen asked? Yeah, punk ass motherfucker. Michael was all over me and he wouldn't get off of me for a second. Girl, he's a trip; that's a nigger for you. I have to go and get ready for work tomorrow, I said to Carmen. I'll talk to you later. Ok, bye.

Two weeks had passed since I have seen or heard from Michael. I felt kind of dizzy and lightheaded. The first thing I thought was, I'm probably pregnant. But no, that can't be. I hope not. Damn it! I told my girlfriend Carmen and she persuaded me to call Michael. I told her no because I wanted to be sure. Let me think about this first.

In the meantime, I called my doctor to schedule an appointment to have a pregancy test done. I could tell my eating habits were starting to change, my breasts were tender, I was vomitting and of all things, I had no cycle. It was definitely late! I went to my doctor's appointment and got examined. Everything was fine and normal. The medical assistant gave me a lab slip to take down to the lab for a blood test for pregnancy. The lab technician told me to call back within an hour or two for the results.

I called back within an hour because I was anxious to know something. When Dr. Miller came on the line, I was nervous as hell. Ms. Simpson, she said. Yes, hi Dr. Miller, I responded. I received the pregancy test back from the lab and your pregnancy test came back positive. You are definitely pregnant. What? I was so shocked! My eyes were buldged and my mouth was wide open. Dr. Miller asked me how I felt. I really couldn't answer her. All I knew was that a baby was growing inside of me and that I was about to become a mother in nine months. What was I going to do? Damn it! I don't want no kid by Michael. We really did not know each other. Shit!

Chapter 5

I couldn't believe I was pregnant. The first person I called was Carmen. I told her that I was six weeks pregnant and that I didn't know what I was going to do. Well Denise, the first thing you need to do, is let Michael know. Yeah, I know. I'll give him a call tomorrow. Before I call him, I need to get my thoughts and feelings together. I'll let you know what the outcome is when I talk to Michael. Goodnight.

I was in deep thought about me being pregnant and about me telling Michael, especially the way it happened. Afterall, Michael always told me he was the only one out of his friends that didn't have a child. So he should be happy, right? Whatever happened to the "I love you, let's get married and then plan for a child?" I didn't even like Michael like that.

I called Michael. When he picked up, I panicked. Hi Michael, it's me, Denise. What's up, he asked? I have some very important news to tell you. What is it, Michael asked nonchalantly? I think he is still pissed with me. But whatever. With his tone of voice, I knew this wasn't going to be good at all. Yeah, what is it Denise? Here goes, I thought.

I went to my doctor's office to take a pregnancy test. When I called for the results, it was positive which means I'm pregnant. There was a long pause on the other end. H-E-L-L-O, are you there Michael, I asked? Yes, I'm here. Well aren't you going to say something? So why are you calling me? What do you mean why am I calling you? Michael, don't act stupid! Well, are you going to say something or not, I asked? Something like what, he replied. Like, how do you feel, are you happy, sad, confused? The next thing I heard in my ear was a click and a dial tone. I said to myself, I can't believe this asshole hung up in my face. For an educated brother, he sure was an ignorant one. I called Michael right back, but he wouldn't take my phone calls. I freaked out. I called Carmen and told her what had just happened. You mean that stupid motherfucker didn't say anything, he just hung up in your face, Carmen asked? Yeah girl, that's about the size of it. I can't believe him Carmen. Me either, Carmen said. Just can't stand up like a real man and face responsibility. He put himself in this position. Why didn't he realize the possibility of pregancy when he forced himself on you, Carmen asked? Dumb ass? Well I'll call him next week to give him some time to think about everything. As far as I'm concerned, Carmen said, there's nothing to think about and he's going to be a father and that's just the bottom line. True that, I replied.

The following week I called Michael again. Hi Michael, it's Denise. What do you want, he asked? Did you have time to think about what I told you? No, I did not. Denise, you can't be serious. But I am, Michael. Ok, here's the scoop. You can't have the baby. Whoa, whoa! Hold up, wait a minute! Why not, I asked? Because right now I'm in a lot of trouble. What kind of trouble, I asked? The RoughNecks are after me. Who? Have you heard of them, he asked? No, I haven't. This is some bullshit, I thought to myself. And besides, what does that have to do with me? These guys are dangerous and they are out to kill me and whoever is around me or involved with me will be killed also. Therefore, they will end up killing you and the baby too. Oh I don't believe that nonsense. That's sounds like a crazy made up story. I don't believe that shit you're telling me. You're fucking lying Michael. Something's up with you. Look girl, I told you right now I'm in big trouble and you can't have the baby. Are you suggesting that I have an abortion? Yes, that's exactly what I am suggesting. Hell no, I blurted out. That's out of the question. "Look, Denise, I'm telling you, if you have that baby, you will be having it alone. I will not be there. I'm not having anything to do with that." I'm in big trouble right now and I have to get it straightened out. As a matter of fact, one of the guys keyed my car. They messed up the lock and scratched my car. I ignored that part. I want to know why would someone want to kill me and an innocent baby? Michael said because again for the third time, if you are involved with me, they will kill you just for being involved with me. Damn, I even had to cut all of my friends off from me. Michael is a clown. He needs an Academy Award for this one. This is a joke. I can't believe this is happening and the stupid ass story Michael was telling me. You know I don't believe a damn word you are saying, right Michael? I can't fucking believe this. Who gives a fuck what you believe, Denise. "All I am telling you is that there is no way in hell you can have that baby and like I said, if you do, you will definitely be on your own and having that baby all by yourself." "I am not involved with any of that and I am not having anything to do with that baby." "Hey asshole, listen to me." "Who in the hell do you think you are?" "And what is your damn problem?" "You sound so stupid and your reasoning is just off the chain!" "This is no movie – this is life." "Michael, how am I supposed to explain this dumb ass shit to my mother or friends for that matter?" Certainly not with the bullshit story line you just gave me. Michael ignored that and said, that's not my problem. That's your problem to deal with and to figure out. You got it, Denise? I have to go. I have a customer. Click. He just hung up in my face. Well fuck you too, I said. I hung up and began to cry and to think about my next move.

As weeks and weeks went on, I tried calling Michael at work. All I would get from his coworkers was: He's busy, he's with a customer, he's gone for the day, he's at lunch and he's on the other line. If I ask to hold for him, no one would never come back to the phone. Neither did Michael. And if I called back and if he answered, once he knew it was me, he would hang up in my face! I couldn't believe that he would treat me like this. Was this some kind of payback because of what went down at my house the very first time he came to see me? I just did not get this.

Finally, one day I spoke with Michael. I told him that I would get the abortion, but first I needed to talk to him face-to-face. Michael sound like he was happy about what I just said as if his dream has come true for him. He agreed to come over to my house. When Michael came over, I told him that I really didn't want to have the abortion, but that I would. He comforted me and told me that the timing is off and that if it is meant for us to be together down the road we will and at that time maybe we can have another baby, but this was definitely not the time. When he left, we both agreed on the abortion, which was to take place on the following Saturday. Michael, can you come with me? Sorry Denise, but I can't. Just can't go. Sorry. I just looked at him and frowned in disgust. This is some unbelievable shit I'm hearing.

On Saturday, I went to Hefner Associates for the abortion. They took my blood, give me a urine test to make sure I was actually pregnant and then they had a counselor talk to me about the procedure. The counselor explained everything to me and told me she was going to leave me alone to get undressed. I undressed and came out into a room full

25

with other females waiting for their names to be called. I got scared. I was about to put my clothes back on and leave, but I didn't.

When the medical assistant called my name, I got up and followed her. She instructed me to sit on the bed. I got on the bed and the doctor examined my cervix. The doctor explained to me that he will have an anesthesiologist give me the anesthesia to put me asleep and then he will start the procedure, which would only take about ten to fifteen minutes. At that moment, I jelled up and changed my mind. The doctor saw that I was nervous and confused about what was happening and about the fact that I was about to have an abortion. Therefore, the doctor suggested that I go home to think about it a little longer before making a decision because once it's done, it's done. I hurried up and put my clothes back on. I knew when I walked out of that abortion clinic on that Saturday, I wasn't coming back.

When I got home, I decided to give Donna a call. Donna is a good friend of Michael's roommate Randy and she knows Michael from college. Hi Donna, it's Denise. How are you doing? Good, Donna replied.

What's up, girl? I have a question to ask you. Do you know if your friend Randy knows anything about Michael being in some kind of trouble with these so called gang bangers called the RoughNecks? Excuse me! What? Donna laughed. I'm sorry Denise but this is the most ridiculous thing I have ever heard. I know Donna this sounds crazy because it is crazy. But this is what Michael told me. I'm pregnant and he says I can't have the baby because these guys are after him and that he can't be involved with anyone because their lives will be in danger as well. Denise, I don't know about that and that is news to me. Is Michael acting like an ass because of you being pregnant? Yes. Let me get in touch with Randy and ask him about this. This is sick Denise. Yes, it is and it is crazy. A crazy made up story by Michael for whatever reasons he have. Why is Michael acting like that? I told Donna what was going on and all. I think Michael is playing games with you, but I will check it out. I'll call you back, Donna said.

The next week Michael changed his number at home, therefore, I could no longer reach him after working hours. I tried him at work again. Peoples Bank, Michael speaking, how may I help you? The minute he heard my voice and I tried talking to him, he cut me off by giving me the same old line. Then out of nowhere he tells me that he's busy right now and that he can't talk. This is very important to me, I said. Well, you'll have to call me another time. I don't have time for this! Then I heard a click. Son of a bitch! I didn't know what to do or who to call, so I decided that I would call Donna back again. Hey Donna, did you find anything out from your friend Randy? Yeah. I talked to Randy and he said as far as he knows, Michael isn't in any kind of trouble and that no so called gang bangers called the RoughNecks are after him. Randy said if that was true they would have heard about it and that Michael wouldn't have a damn thing to worry about with all the frat brothers he have. Thanks for the info, Donna. No problem and keep me informed. I will, I said. So, this nigger tried to get me to terminate my baby under false pretense? What a low down dirty dog! Well I have news for him. It ain't happening.

I couldn't figure out why Michael was lying and what is the real deal. I decided to call the ob/gyn department at the clinic to set up my first prenatal visit. Within a week, I was at my first prenatal visit. When I arrived, I was asked to fill out a medical history form. The form asked all kinds of questions about my health and Michael's health. I couldn't tell them anything about Michael's health because I didn't know anything. Once the forms were filled out, the medical assistant came to me and told me that she needed me to go into the ladies room to give a urine sample in the cup she had given me and once I'm done to go into Room 3C, get undressed from the waist down and then the doctor will come in to see me.

A few minutes later, there was a knock on the door. Come in, I said. The door opened. Hi, I'm Dr. Goldberg and I will be your doctor throughout your pregancy. I smiled. Hello, I said. Ok, let's get started. Are you having any kind of problems so far, he asked? No. Are you feeling any discomfort in the pelvic area? No. What about any spotting? No. Great, everything seems to be going fine at this point. How are your eating habits? They're good. Step on the scale and let me weigh you. Dr. Goldberg said I weighed in at one hundred and forty five pounds. "Dang," I said! Does the father know about the baby and how does he feel about it? I told Dr. Goldberg that Michael knew, but he wasn't happy about it at all. He'll come around, Dr. Goldberg said. Lay down on your back and let me examine you and check the baby's heartbeat. I was excited about hearing my baby's heartbeat. Everything feels fine. The heartbeat is definitely a strong one.

As I got dressed to leave my appointment, I realized for the first time in weeks, I felt some relief of happiness. I went to work feeling good. I went to my boss, Paul and told him I needed to speak with him. Let's go into a conference room, he suggested. As soon as I closed the door to the conference room, I just came right out with it. "Paul, I'm pregnant," I told him. "Oh really, is that so?" "Yep, really, it is so." We both started laughing. Congratulations, Denise. "Thank you," I said. Let me know if there is anything that me or the team can do for you. Thanks Paul, I will. By the way, can you get me accommodations for two nights at the Biltmore Hotel in Providence, RI for Monday and Tuesday. No problem, Paul. I'm off to a meeting, he said. Hey, Denise. Yeah. I'm really happy for you and I mean that. I exhaled and then smiled. Thanks.

When Paul left for his meeting, I decided to call Michael hoping his dumb ass would decide to listen to me. May I speak to Michael please, I asked? Sure, who's calling please? This is Denise Simpson. One moment please, the teller said. The teller came back to the phone only to say that Michael is with a customer. Would you like to leave a message? No, I'll try him later. Click. I said to myself, Michael's still playing those silly games. I waited an hour before calling back. This time he was gone for the day.

I called Carmen. "Hello," she answered. "It's me, Denise." You know I tried calling Michael three times today and each time I called, the tellers claimed that he was with a customer or he had left for the day. Carmen paused and said to me, "Denise, I'll telling you straight out, Michael's bullshitting you around." I bet he is at his fucking job. Hold on, Carmen said. She called him on her three way line. Good afternoon, Peoples Bank, the voice answered. Is Michael available? Who's speaking? Angela Wilkins, she lied. One moment please. Within a matter of seconds, Michael came to the phone.

Hello, can I help you, he said? Yeah, you can. Why the fuck are you hanging up on Denise and why won't you talk to her when you know she's pregnant and she needs to speak with you? Look Carmen, mind your own fucking business. It is my business because Denise is a good friend of mine. Michael started going off and he told Carmen not to call his damn job anymore. The next second or so, Carmen started going off on him. She told Michael that he was full of shit. Before you know it, he hung up in her face. Carmen was talking to a dead line.

I just don't believe that sucker, no good bastard. He's a coward and he's definitely not a man. I told you everytime I call, he hangs up on me. Michael has a serious problem, Carmen suggested. He's definitely hiding something from you. But what could it be, I asked? I couldn't tell you girl. Well I know one thing, I don't believe that shit about some RoughNecks being after him. Something is not right, I said to Carmen.

What time will you be home? About six thirty, I said. Call me then. Alright.

I was so busy talking to Carmen on the phone for an hour, I forgot to set up hotel reservations for my boss and also the Executive Committee Meetings. What the hell, I thought. It's late in the day. I'll do it first thing tomorrow morning.

When I got home, I was dead tired. I cooked, ate, took a shower and then tried to take a nap. Just then, the phone rang. I was hoping it was Michael, but it wasn't. It was my mother. I was just calling to see how you was doing, she said. Oh, I was just about to take a nap. Where's Tameka, I asked? Tameka is my little sister. She stayed afterschool. Oh ok. Oh mom, before we hang up, I have something to tell you. Hold on, that's my other line. Hello, I answered. Hey Denise, whatcha doing? Hey Marcy, can I call you back in a little while? Sure no problem, she said. I need to hip you to what's going on. I clicked back to the other line. Mom, I'm back. That was Marcy calling. Guess what, I said to my mother. What, she answered. I'm pregnant! By who? Michael, I said. How far are you, she asked? About eight weeks. What are your plans? Well if you're wondering if I'm going to have the baby, the answer is yes. How does Michael feel about it? I don't know yet. He's acting stupid at the moment. What I really wanted to say was that he's acting like a jerk. Hold on again, Mom. Hello. It was Marcy again. She was anxious to hear what I had to tell her. Marcy, let me get my mom off the other line. Mom, I'll talk to you tomorrow. Ok, love you. Bye. Hello Marcy, I'm back. What's up girl, what's the scoop, she asked? For some reason, Michael isn't taking any of my phone calls. He's refusing to speak to me. When I call him at work, he tells his coworkers to say he's either busy or has left for the day. Always some kind of excuse or lie being told. I know he's there when I call. Denise, you better believe they are lying for him. Did you tell your mother? Yeah, but I couldn't tell her how much of a jerk and asshole Michael is being right now. You know you can't keep it hidden for too long. I know. Marcy, what time is it, I asked? About eleven. I got to get off of this phone. You know tomorrow is another work day. So much for a nap. I need a good night sleep. Ok then, I'll talk to you tomorrow. Goodnight, girl.

Chapter 6

I slept like a baby last night. Thank God it's Saturday. I got out of bed and went into the bathroom. I took a long hard look at myself in the mirror, realizing my face was getting fatter and my stomach was starting to bulge. The cool shower felt good on this hot eighty degree morning. I made myself some breakfast. God, it's a beautiful day, what can I do? I couldn't exactly call Michael, since he was still acting shitty. I decided to give my mother a call. I told my mother that I would come down to visit her and my little sister Tameka.

I made it down to my mother's house around three thirty in the afternoon. I ranged the doorbell and got buzzed in. Hi mom, I said? What's up, Tameka? Are you all cooking out today? Yeah, my mother responded. It's too damn hot to cook inside, especially when I don't have an air conditioner. Tameka looked at me and said, "your face is fat and your butt is getting a little too big." Must be having a girl, my mother said. Well, I'm almost four months. I feel fine and the baby's heartbeat is strong and stable. What about Michael, my mother asked? You should call him and tell him to take you to get some ice cream, she said. Michael went to visit his mother in Chicago this weekend, I lied. Why didn't you go? Well, you know, I didn't feel like that twelve to thirteen hour drive. But Denise, this is the time you two should be spending time together, not apart. We will, Mom. Just don't start feeding into anything more than what it really is. Let's go outside, I said.

After we started the fire on the grill, we put chicken wings, beef ribs, hamburgers and hotdogs on the grill. I had a plate full of food as if this was the first time I've ever eaten. When we were through, we cleaned up our mess, talked, laughed and then my mother and sister drove me home. As I got out of the car and walked towards my building, I shouted, thanks for the ride home. I'll see you guys in church tomorrow.

When I woke up, it was 11:00 a.m. Oh shit! I'm late for church. Well, I'll go next Sunday. I can't be rushing around like that. All day I lounged around the house, ate like a pig, watched cable and slept. I was in a deep sleep when I heard the phone rang. Hi Denise, it's Carmen. What's up? "Are you asleep," she asked? "Yes I was," I responded. "Michael called?" "Nope." "Ignorant and stupid." I chuckled at Carmen's comment. At this point Carmen, I don't think he will. Maybe you should try calling him again tomorrow at work. I know Carmen, but I don't want to get my feelings hurt again. Just try and see what happens. Denise when you look at it, you can't be any worse off than you are now. You're right, tomorrow I will try again.

I went to work early on Monday morning, feeling well rested. Suddenly for the first time, I felt my baby move. It felt weird, but I liked it. Today is going to be a slow day since Paul will be in Providence today and tomorrow. I'll get my work done, go to lunch, then give Michael a call. By 3:00 p.m. I was bored at work. I decided I would call Carmen before I call Michael. Carmen, it's Denise. What's up, she asked? I'm about to call Michael and I'm kind of nervous. Don't be Denise. If Michael talks to you, just ask him why he's doing what he is doing and beg him if you have to and get him to talk to you face-to-face. Ok, Carmen. Here's goes. Wish me luck.

Frankly, I didn't have enough guts to call Michael when I got off the phone with Carmen, so I decided to call Marcy to get her opinion. Marcy asked how I was doing and all. I told Marcy that I wanted to ask her a question. "Do you think I should try calling Michael once more," I asked? Yes, she said. Don't be afraid Denise, you have every right. Then I started to cry. I know what you're saying Marcy, but I'm afraid he will hang up in my face again. You won't know that for sure Denise if you don't try. I know, I said. Alright, Marcy. I will call him right now and I'll call you back to let you know how I made out. And Marcy, thanks for listening and being a good friend. We said our goodbyes.

"Good afternoon, Peoples Bank, Michael speaking," may I help you? I paused before I spoke. My heart was beating so fast. "Michael," I said. "Please don't hang up, just listen for a minute." "Can we please talk?" "Please listen to me and what I have to say." "That's all I am asking of you." "Don't hang up in my face again," please. "I'm begging you." I know you want me to have an abortion for some strange reason or another. Yep, that's right, Denise, I do. That's exactly what I want you to do. Like I told you, right now I'm in a lot of trouble and this is definitely the wrong time for this to be happening. Michael, what do you mean it's the best thing to do? I have already explained myself to you, he said. The bottom line is that you just can't have this baby. I won't and can't be there for you or for the baby. I know it is a horrible thing to say but it's for real. I can't put it any other way. Let's just get this problem solved so we can both move on from this. Well it's too late now, so let's just compromise Michael. If you come over and really tell me what's going on, I will go to New York to get an abortion. But I need to know what is going on so I can be comfortable in the decision I am making. There is a clinic in New York that performs abortions up to the fifth or six month of pregnancy. After we talk, I will plan to go to New York to take care of this. Ok, deal he said. I'll see you tomorrow evening. Isn't this something, I thought. You mean to tell me that Michael doesn't give a damn if I risk my life by terminating my preganancy this late in the game? How cold hearted can he be? That's cold and very selfish of Michael. I thought to myself, what kind of person is Michael? This can't be because of what happened at my house. Something just doesn't sit too well with me. I can't put my finger on it, but something is just not right. Please God, give me or show me a sign of what is going on. An hour after I came home from work, Carmen and Marcy were in front of my door. They asked me if I'd gotten anywhere with Michael. I told them, not really but he agreed to come over tomorrow evening. That's a piece of good news, Marcy said. It's about time that asshole is coming to his senses, Carmen said. I wouldn't read too much into this if I were you all. I mean, Michael is still singing the same song and wants me to terminate the pregnancy, even though it puts my life in jeopardy at this stage of the game. Ugh, I can't stand him said Carmen! Anyway, we were in the neighborhood and decided to stop by for a few just to see your cute, pudgy face. Ha, you all are a trip. Well now that we have seen you, Marcy said, we have to get going. Alrighty then, I will talk to you guys later. Bye, baby girl.

I thought myself how good it felt to come home and relax without a headache for once. After I got to work and got settled, the first thing I did was call Michael to make sure that he is still coming over this evening to talk. He said he was and that he will see me in a little bit. Cool.

I was so nervous. I couldn't even eat like I wanted to. I called Carmen and Marcy. They both told me to relax, to be calm and to make sure I ask all the right questions. Around 7:45 p.m. my doorbell rings. I answered. It was Michael. I buzzed him in. Then there was the knock on my door. Suddenly, Michael appeared right in front of me. Michael looked good but had a crazed look in his eyes. Like he was possessed or something. He came in and I offered him to have a seat. Blountly, he mentioned that he would stand because he wouldn't be staying long. The nerve of him. I frowned at him and was looking at him like he had two heads or something. Michael then put his hands on my shoulders. He told me how sorry he was and then started with that bullshit again about not having the baby and these damn RoughNecks. I don't want to get you involved, he said. "Oh, so I'm supposed to have an abortion just like that." Michael didn't say a word. "Answer me damn it," I shouted! Denise, I love you. Fuck off, will you, I screamed! "You don't even know me!" Denise, we can always have another baby. Now is just not the right time. Trust me, Denise. For one Michael, you are definitely not to be trusted. Your words mean nothing at all. So Michael, save the bullshit for someone else because you know damn well I don't buy into what you are telling me. There's something wrong and there's something that you're not telling me. Michael went into this thing about having to go to Chicago to see about his mom. Another damn lie. I got so frustrated that I told him that I would call the clinic in New York and have the abortion. I can't come with you though, Michael said. What? Why not, I asked? Because my mother is sick and I need all of my money to go visit her in Chicago. Are you going to at least help pay for it, I asked? I can't Denise because I need all of my money. Ok, get the fuck out of my face and out of my house! When Michael left, he wished me luck on the abortion. I slammed the door behind his dumb ass. The nerve of his black ass.

The abortion was scheduled for next Saturday. I am supposed to leave that Friday afternoon to go to New York. The night before I was to leave for New York, I was instructed not to eat or drink anything after twelve midnight, due to the fact that I was scheduled to have general anesthesia. When I got up on Saturday, I was starving like hell. I showered and my mother and I got ready head to New York. You sure this is what you want to do, my mother asked? Yes, I said. I don't want to have a baby and have to end up raising it all by myself. I want this baby to have a mother and a father. I really don't understand Michael, she said. One thing I told my mother that I was sure about was that after today, Michael is out of my life for good and he will NEVER in his lifetime see me again! He could fuck off and die for all I care.

As we walked towards the entrance of the abortion clinic, protestors were in front of the door with signs of a baby's head dismantled from the body, a heart, arms and legs being torn apart by a suction machine. The protestors were also yelling things such as "your baby has a heartbeat and is alive, don't kill an innocent child, we'll help you, that's murder and your mother didn't kill you." I got depressed and sickened to my stomach at that moment.

When I walked into that clinic with my mother, I had a feeling I wasn't going for it. I think we drove all the way to New York for nothing. All kinds of thoughts were going through my mind, particularly the ones that the protestors were saying outside of the clinic. I went to the reception desk to sign in. I told them that my appointment is at 10:00 a.m. I filled out paper work, returned them to the receptionist and was instructed to go to the lab. After the lab work was done, a counselor came to talk to me. As I was being counseled, I told the lady that I changed my mind. There's no way I'm going through this, I said. I couldn't think of having my unborn child being suctioned out of me with a suction machine. No way. Hell no! I don't need that shit in my life! Fuck no. This is out of the question. I would not be able to live with myself. I got up, went to the waiting room to instruct my mom for us to leave and I was out of there! I could hear the lady at the front desk calling my name. We kept walking to the car. I did not look back for any reason whatsoever. I want no memory of that clinic.

When my mother and I left the clinic, I felt good and relieved. We went straight to IHOP for breakfast. Damn, I was starved. I through down like someone who was starving to death.

We left IHOP and got on the freeway and headed back home. Once I got dropped off at home, I called my girls. Marcy and Carmen were both happy and glad that I didn't go through the abortion at such a late stage in the pregnancy. All three of us were rejoicing. Too bad for Michael. You'll be fine. I had to laugh at myself. Carmen with her crazy self starting singing, "Michael's gonna be a daddy, Michael's gonna be a daddy." We all fell out with laughter.

"What happened when you and your mom got to New York," Marcy asked? I just chickened out and changed my mind, I told her. "What will I say to Michael?" He thinks I had the abortion. "Fuck what you would say to Michael, Marcy blurted out." "Straight up girl, fuck him," Carmen said. He can go jump in the lake and drown for all I care.

When Michael finds this out, he will be pissed. "Who cares how he feels?" "It's not about him, it's about you and what you want." "It's your body and not his." "That's true," I said. I exhaled, let out a chuckle and said, you're right. "Who gives a fuck or cares what Michael would say or think?" I'm tired. Talking about Michael is too stressful and too exhausting for me. I'll talk to you guys later. To hell with Michael and his bullshit. I'm done. Goodnight.

Chapter 7

Hi, Mrs. Simpson, this is Donna. Is Denise there? No, Donna, she's not here, my mother said. Do you want me to have her call you? Yes please, Donna said. Can you let Denise know that it is very important that I talk to her right away? Ok, I will Donna. Thanks.

When I woke up on this beautiful Sunday morning, I sensed something wasn't right. I had the strangest feeling. My stomach was in knots. I felt sick. It wasn't me or had anything to do with the baby. It was something else bugging the hell out of me.

I decided to take the bus over to Carmen's house. When I got there, Carmen was sitting on the porch. "What's up girlfriend," Carmen asked? I just wanted to come over to see if you wanted to go in town. Sure, why not. Let me call my mother and ask her if she needs anything from downtown. Hi mom, what are you doing? Just cooking. In this hot heat, I asked. Yeah, we got to eat, don't we? I suppose so. Where are you? Oh, I'm over Carmen's house. We are on our way downtown and I called you to see if you needed anything from Eckards. Please bring me a box of Tide with Bleach. Ok, I said. By the way, Denise, Donna called. She wants you to call her right away. She says it's important.

Ok, I'll call her before we leave. Carmen, let me give Donna a quick call before we leave. No problem.

Donna, hi. It's Denise. Where have you been, Donna asked anxiously? I have been trying to reach you since early this morning. I'm over to my friend Carmen's house. Why, what's up? Did you go through with the abortion in New York, she asked? No, why? Good. Well, I have some news for you. Ok. When Donna said that, I knew that it had something to do with crazy ass Michael. Are you ready for this, she asked me?

Ready for what, I answered? Michael got married today at 2:00 p.m. at Greater Life Baptist Church. Huh, what? I went quiet and numb for a minute. Donna asked me if I heard her. Yes, I heard you. What, say that again! Nevermind. I heard you clearly. Where did you hear this? Listen, I bumped into a friend of mine who attended the same college as Michael and knows Michael as well. She told me she came up from Philly to attend Michael's wedding. I asked her, Michael Who? She was like Michael Davenport. Apparently, Michael invited her to his wedding. Yeah, it seems that way, doesn't it. I guess Michael did not invite me because he knows that you and I know each other and are friends, Donna said. Ugh! That's a hot mess and Michael is very wrong for that. He should have been up front with you. Now he put you in this crazy situation and he put his wife-to-be in a crazy situation as well. I was stunned and could not speak for a moment. I was in a daze.

I can't believe this is happening. All of this time Michael has been lying to me about some gang bangers called the RoughNecks being after him and drilling me about having an abortion. I got the clear picture now. Michael was living a double life and it caught up with his silly, ignorant ass. He was trying to hook up with me, things happened, I rejected his ass and out of it, I became pregnant. I got caught up in some bullshit. He knew he was getting married and this is why he wanted me to have the abortion. Why couldn't he just be up front? Things could have been handled differently. I wasn't going to just go get an abortion because of what he wanted and especially because of some dumb made up lie he was telling me. This is really messed up. I kept asking Michael over and over why is he treating me like this and all he could say is that he's in a lot of trouble. Well, I'm going up to that church right now. Thanks for the information, Donna. Be careful.

I told Carmen what I had just found out. She told me how sorry she was to hear this. I don't know what to say, Denise, but I do know that Michael is a complete jerk and an idiot. Do you want to come with me to the church? Are you serious Denise, Carmen asked? Yes, as a heart attack. I'll come with you, she said. We can use my sister's car.

As we drove from Carmen's house to the church, I couldn't block out of my mind what Donna had just told me. Carmen, for months Michael's been lying to me. He made up that bullshit story about the RoughNecks and how if he is with me, they would kill me and the baby. "What kind of a person would stoop this low?" All of these fucking lies and games, I screamed! My life is totally screwed. How embarassing.

As we approached the church, we didn't see anyone outside or that many cars for that matter. There has to be someone in there, I thought. Let's pull into the parking lot, I said. Carmen said she would get out and knock on the door. I waited in the car. When I saw Carmen waving for me to get out of the car, I did as she instructed. As I approached Carmen, I could see a man expressing himself to her. I could see that he was saying something serious to Carmen by the look on his face. When I was getting closer to them, I could hear Carmen asking the man if there was a wedding there today at 2:00 p.m. The man said yes. Carmen asked if it was a wedding with someone with the last name of Davenport. I believe so, the man replied. Hold on, he said, let me double check for you. As we waited to hear if it was actually Michael or not, we chatted. I can't believe Michael did this to me. What's wrong with telling the truth so the right decision can be made. At least I could have made a decision whether to continue this pregnancy under the circumstances or to have an abortion under the circumstances. Michael made the choice for me. He didn't even think about me or my feelings, just his very own. Here comes the guy, I said. The man responded by saying "the wedding was definitely a Davenport wedding." Here's a copy of the program. I snatched the program out of the man's hand and when I saw that Michael Davenport was on the program as the groom, I just stood there with my hand over my heart, then I broke down and cried. Carmen thanked the man for his help. As we walked to the car, I fainted. When I woke up, I was in the hospital. There was this nurse standing by my side. She told me that my stress level was very high and I can't afford the stress under my condition. The first thing I wanted to know, was "how's my baby?" "The baby is fine," the nurse responded. Just don't get too stressed out because you could end up doing harm to the baby or possibly end up losing the baby. No, I can't have that. I can't lose my baby. Michael or his bullshit is not worth it.

The next day, Carmen and I went to my mother's house. My mother was asking for the Tide with Bleach. Mom please sit down, I said. We have to talk to you. Are you up to tell your mom this Denise, Carmen asked? No, you can tell her for me? Mrs. Simpson, Carmen began. Yesterday, we found out that Michael got married. What? Yeah, I know but it's true. How could he do this in Denise's condition, she asked? Oh, I'll be ok Mom. I went to the hospital yesterday suffering from a fainting spell, that's why I couldn't bring the detergent. I kept calling you all last night and couldn't get an answer. That's why, I said. Everything is fine and under control. It has to be, I said. The baby's life depends on it. Do you want to stay here tonight, my mother asked. No, I'll be fine. I just want to be alone right now. You know I will always be here for you. I know. I'll call you when I get home. You ready Carmen? Yes. Goodbye Mrs. Simpson. Bye Carmen.

The next morning, I got up and went to work. I couldn't concentrate at all. One person I must call is Kevin, Michael's friend. I dialed the number. Peoples Bank can I help you? "Yes, my I speak with Kevin Johnson?" Hold on please. Hello, this is Kevin. Kevin this is Denise. "What's up girlie girl," Kevin asked? "You know what's up," I said. Don't play. "Your fucked up friend Michael got married yesterday." Kevin tried to lie. Don't even try to lie Kevin because I went up to the church. Kevin said to me, "you wasn't there." "I didn't see you." I got there too late, that's why you didn't see me. I also have the program. As a matter of fact, Kevin you were one of the ushers. So are you still pregnant, he asked? Yes, I most certainly am and you can tell that fucked up friend of yours when he gets back from his fucking honeymoon that his plan to get me to have an abortion failed and back fired in his face. That's all I have to say on the subject. I just clicked on Kevin's ass.

I decided to go out to lunch. In my travels, I bumped into an old friend of mine name Sandra. I haven't seen you in years Sandra. It's so good to see you. I haven't seen you in so long either, Sandra said to me. Oh, I've been around. How have you been Denise? Pretty good. Guess what? I'm expecting a baby. I smiled. Really, she said. You don't even look it. How far are you? Four and a half months. You know that guy Michael I always told you about? Yeah. Well he's the father and he is really messed up in the mind and got life really messed up. Huh? Anyway, he got married on me this past weekend. To who, Sandra wanted to know? Anyone we know? I don't know who she is but here is the program. Sandra snatched the program out of my hand and began

43

analyzing the program. No way Denise. I know this girl. What, you do? How? Yeah, she's from the projects and my mother and her mother are good friends. I looked at Sandra with a frown on my face like she was on drugs or something. I asked her if she attended the wedding and she said no. I knew she was getting married though. This is a trip! That's really messed up. You don't have to remind me girl. Come to think of it Denise, I knew Karen was getting married to a guy name Michael, I just didn't know, Michael who. What a coincidence, Sandra said. If I knew this person, I would confront her and let her know the deal. Sandra then said, I don't want to get in the middle of this drama, but her mother works at Dillards. She's the only black woman in her department. She's kind of tall and wears a short haircut. Go and talk to her, just don't mention my name to her. I won't Sandra. Thanks for your help. I dashed off to Dillards. It's on now.

As I walked through the crowded floor of Dillards, I could see and smell all the expensive leather handbags and perfumes. I approached the escalators and went to the fifth floor. I was definitely nervous. Thinking to myself I asked, "do I really want to do this?" I don't want to start no drama with these people I do not know. Then I remembered that someone had to know what was going on. Who better to drop the bomb on Michael's new mother-in-law, but me. The first person I saw in the department was a white haired woman. I asked her if she could tell me where I can find Mrs. Richards.

She pointed to a black woman who was talking on the phone. "Thank you," I said. While I was waiting to drop the bomb, I could hear Mrs. Richards yacking away on the phone about her daughter's wedding. I said to myself, "I wish she would hurry up so I can drop my bomb on her and get the hell out of there." When I get through telling her what I have to tell her, she won't be so happy-go-lucky about her daughter's wedding and marriage to Michael. I really didn't want to bust her bubble, but damn it, I needed to be heard. Finally, I heard her put the receiver down. My heart was racing.

I went over to her and asked her if she is Mrs. Richards? She looked at me with an attitude, half smile and a frowned face and said, "yes I am." "Mrs. Richards, my name is Denise." "I know you don't know who I am." "You're right, I don't," she said. Gee, she's harder than I thought. "First of all, Mrs. Richards, there is something you need to know about your daughter." "Which one because I have three," she asked? "I'm talking about the one that just got married." "What about her?" This woman had a nasty attitude. I did nothing to her. I started to explain.

"I understand your daughter, Karen got married to Michael Davenport." "Yes, that's correct," she answered. "Well I've known Michael for a while and we have been involved to a certain extent." "What does this have to do with my daughter Karen," she asked? "Well for one, Michael and I are expecting a baby." "Michael knows about it." "He lied to me to keep me from finding out and he tried to get me to have an abortion." "He never told me that he was engaged to be married." "All Michael said to me was that he was in a lot of trouble and these guys were after him." At this point, Mrs. Richards was looking at me in shock. I explained to her that I was sorry for coming up to her job and dropping the bomb on her. I thanked her for her time and for listening to me, then I left. I'm sorry, but she had to know so it can get back to her daughter Karen. Michael sure as hell wasn't going to tell her. Michael started it, so I am going to finish it. I am going to show his ass what fucking with me can be like.

I headed by back to work after leaving Dillards and then called Carmen. I explained what I had just done and Carmen was happy. "Denise, I'm glad you told Michael's mother-in-law." "Serves him right," she said. "What kind of a guy would get you pregnant, abandon you and his unborn child, then run off and get married on you, Carmen asked?" "When Michael and I met, I thought he was a single man. "That's how he portrayed himself to be and there were no signs of another woman or at least I didn't see any signs." "He was always available." I had no clue. "He knew what he was planning with this other woman, but I didn't." "Well he fucked himself, Carmen said." I hope he rots in hell. "Yeah me too," I said.

Chapter 8

I went to my prenatal visit. Dr. Goldberg came in the room. How are you today, Denise? I feel pretty good. Any problems I should know about, he asked? Nope. Dr. Goldberg asked me why didn't I bring the father along? To be honest, Dr. Goldberg, the father ran out on me and got married on me. He told me he didn't want anything to do with me or the baby. Have you tried contacting him, Dr. Goldberg asked? Nope, not lately. I started to cry. Here's a kleenex. Thank you, I said. Dr. Goldberg ask me if I was willing to see a family counselor. I agreed. I was given a referral form. I was referred to a family counselor by the name of Dr. Palmer.

Two weeks later, I was sitting in the family counseling unit. I waited as my name was called. Dr. Palmer will see you now, Ms. Simpson. I got out of my seat and there stood this small built woman with dark brown hair standing at the desk, with a white lab coat on. Hi I'm Dr. Palmer, she said. Are you Denise? Yes, I am. Follow me please.

I followed Dr. Palmer into her office. The first thing we discussed was the pregnancy and how I was doing. She asked me about Michael. I told her the whole story in big sobs and tears. Try not to get yourself all choked up about this. Everything will work out. Michael is just being a jerk right now. I feel he will come around. I told Dr. Palmer that I didn't think he would. Michael has made it very clear to me that if I have this baby, he wanted nothing to do with the baby or me. Did he tell you he was getting married, she asked? No he did not. All he said was that some gang was after him and if I have the baby they would kill me and the baby. Dr. Palmer was looking at me as to say, "is this guy a sicko or what?" "Did you believe him," she asked? "No, I didn't." "And, I had no clue he was getting married." "Are you going to try to contact Michael?" "No, I'm going to leave it alone." "I have done all I could do." I am mentally and emotionally drained from this whole ordeal. Everytime I called Michael in the past months at work and if he answered the phone, he would hang up on me. Or if one of his coworkers answered, they would lie by saying he's with a customer or on the other line. "This is a bunch of crap," Dr. Palmer. She agreed with me.

Denise, "this is what I'll suggest to you." Wait until the baby is born, then write Michael a letter telling him you had the baby and you would like to talk to him. Make sure you send the letter certified, that way you'll know if not Michael, then someone in the office received and signed for it and at least gave it to him. I have a feeling after the baby is born, Michael will want to see the baby. This will conclude our session for today. Call me if you need to see me again. I will Dr. Palmer and thanks for the time and advice. No problem she said. It's my job.

After I left the session with Dr. Palmer, I felt much better that someone listened to me and could sympathize with me. I began to see some light at the end of the tunnel. I had finally opened up and let all hell break loose. All the things I had held inside of me for so long were no longer there. When I went to work, I was happy. When I got home, I showered, ate dinner and then relaxed. I felt great. I even had a smile on my face for once. I could feel that God was with me through this ordeal and would not leave me nor forsake me.

I checked the messages that were left on my answering service. I didn't bother to return any of my phone calls. However, I called my mother before I turned in for the night. We talked for a few minutes. She told me not to worry, but to be strong and try to make the best of it and move on. We said goodnight to each other and hung up. I stayed up an half hour more reading. Finally, I dosed off into a deep, deep sleep.

Chapter 9

The phone was ringing. It was Carmen. What's up Carmen, I asked? Nothing. I was calling to let you know that I'm heading back to Miami next week. You are, I asked in amazement? Yeah, but just for a short while. My mother wants me to help her out with the hotel business down there. You better let me know when you're leaving. Don't leave without me seeing you first. I won't. You know Denise, I really hate to leave you in a condition like this. Oh, don't worry about me, I'm due in a couple of weeks. Homegirl, believe me, I will be fine.

I was so tired. The following week at work was long, aggravating and tiring. I could not wait until 5:00 p.m. to come. I noticed everyone in the office started acting funny around 4:30 p.m. Michele, who is a white coworker of mine came over to me and said, "Denise, I'll drop you off at home today." I thought to myself, she's tripping! For all Michele knew I could be living in the ghetto with all kinds of drugs, prostitution and crack houses going on and yet she wants to drive me home. It just didn't make any sense to me. I was a little curious, but I said ok anyway.

It was a little after 5:00 p.m. and I couldn't find Michele. I'm ready to go home. "Where's Michele," I asked Rena? "She's down the hall."

Denise, Rena said, "did you know that we are having a very important meeting at 5:15 p.m. and it's mandatory?" "No," I didn't. "Since when?" This is the first I've heard of it too. Shit, I am ready to go home. I'm tired. What the hell? Why is the meeting being held after 5:00 p.m.? Don't they know we are out of here by then? Let's just check it out anyway since we are still here. Rena and I left our work stations heading towards the conference room.

When Rena opened the door to the conference room, everyone yelled "SURPRISE!" I was shocked and tears started filling my eyes. I couldn't believe it. No wonder Michele wanted to drive me home. Paul said, "you didn't think we would let you leave the bank without having a baby shower for you, did you?" With your fiesty self, he added. I just rolled my eyes and smiled at him. Oh, this is so sweet. Thank you all so much!

After we ate, I opened my gifts. I got a Fisher Price high chair, a car seat and lots of receiving blankets and sleepers. I was amazed to see how much my my coworkers really cared. It was very touching. They have the slightest clue of what I'm going through. Michele asked me if I was ready to go? I said yes. Once the gifts were packed up and taken to Michele's car, I hugged my coworkers and they wished me all the luck for a safe delivery. Once Michele and I got inside of my apartment, we put the gifts in the room. Wow, this is a beautiful nursery. Thanks. Well, Denise, I need to get going. I walked with Michele down to the lobby. We hugged and said our goodbyes. Looking at myself in the mirror, I realized I was huge. I weighed myself which displayed one hundred seventy pounds. And my nose! Man, it was so big that it looked like a clown's nose. It just wasn't red. I thought to myself, once the baby is born, I will lose it. I was due in a few weeks. Thank God. I'm ready. Whew!

Everyday I ate fruit and Mrs. Fields cookies, hoping the baby would come. When I went to my doctor's appointment on Thursday, he examined me and told me that I was only one and a half centimeters. I asked Dr. Goldberg if I would have the baby today and he said maybe by Saturday. You are all set for now Denise, he said. Make an appointment to see me the day after tomorrow. I did just that.

That night I decided to stay over my mother's house. I knew any day now the baby would be coming. The next morning I woke up, I felt kind of crampy. When I got in the shower, I got my first contraction. I hopped out of the shower so fast. I dried off and put my clothes on. "Mom, mom." I screamed! I think it's time for me to go to the doctor's office. I'm in labor! I called the doctor's office and was instructed to come in right away. I reached the clinic. Immediately, I was called. Dr. Goldberg came into the room. Well Denise, let's examine you. He chuckled. Yesterday you were only one and a half centimeters and today you are five centimeters. I asked Dr. Goldberg what does that mean? He simply said, "you're going to have your baby today." Oh shit. I panicked. I was scared.

I arrived at the hospital in an ambulance. My mother was right there by my side. I was wheeled into the admissions office. They checked me in and logged in all of my information - such as date of admission, time of admission and the prognosis. Once all this was taken care of, I was taken to the labor and delivery unit. My heart was pumping. I was scared and nervous. It's natural. This is my first baby.

The nurse came in the room where I was. I was instructed to take everything off and to put all of my belongings in the hospital bag that was handed to me. I also was given a gown to put on.

I got into the hospital bed. I was examined by the doctor that was on duty. She told me that she had to break my water, which she did. The monitor was strapped to my stomach. This way my contractions would be monitored and the baby's heartbeat. Shortly after this, the doctor came in to examine me again. She told me that I was eight centimeters. I was in my final stages of labor. Damn, that was fast. Dr. Fine asked me if I wanted anesthesia because now was the time. I told her no. It was weird because the contractions I was having were crampy. They weren't that painful at all to me. I thought I was going to have labor pains that would seem to last a lifetime according to some of my friends experiences with childbirth. One of the other doctors told me when he returns, it should be time for me to start pushing. An half hour went by again. I was examined, which seemed for the twentieth time. The doctor said to me, "Denise, you are ten centimeters; it's time to start pushing." My eyes opened so wide. I don't know why I started looking at my mother, as to ask her to help me. Of all times, this was the one time she couldn't do a damn thing for me. I was on my own. The nurses and doctors kept telling me when the next contraction comes, they wanted me to count to ten by holding my breath and then push as hard as I can. I did everything they told me to do. Ok, ok, said one nurse. I can see a whole bunch of black hair. Denise, the doctor said, if you push on your next contraction really hard, the baby will slide out. I think my mind went blank because I had looked at the table on the other side of me and noticed that there was this huge size needle. I forgot about what the doctor had just said to me. I asked the doctors if I would have to get a needle. They responded by saying only if the baby rips you. I guess the baby did rip me because the next thing I knew, I pushed really hard and all of a sudden I felt this hard pinch from that fucking needle, which was stuck right into the vaginal area. I screamed so loud that the baby just slid on out. It's over, it's over, they shouted. It's a baby girl! It's a baby girl! The nurse put the baby on my chest, then took her off, washed her and wrapped her and then gave my baby to my mother. I turned my head towards my mother and looked at my newborn baby girl. She is so beautiful.

While being stitched, the doctor told me that my daughter was healthy, she weighed six pounds-six ounces and that all her body parts were in tact. I was so happy.

The baby was taken up to the nursery. They kept me in the delivery room a little while longer so I could get cleaned up. When I got up to the floor, I wanted to hold my daughter but I couldn't because I had a slight fever.

Finally, the nurse brought the baby to me. I held her and kissed her. She was so little, cute and kind of chunky. I fed her the Similac with iron, changed her, held her some more and let her sleep in the bed with me. I didn't let my daughter go back into the nursery, only when the pediatrician needed to check her or to do blood work. After all I've been through, I wasn't taking any chances. I named my daughter, Alexis Reneé Simpson.

The next day, I received a lot of phone calls and visitors. Kevin, Michael's friend, had the nerve to come visit me. Can you believe that? I think he was just being nosey. He looked at Alexis and said to me, Denise, she looks just like Michael. I told Kevin, well you can do me a favor and tell your friend that he has a newborn baby girl, whether he likes it or not.

I went home that Sunday. It was cold outside. The doctors told me to take care and what to do if this or that happens to the baby. It felt strange going home with a newborn baby. My life has just changed. I was a mother. I had to not only look out for myself, but for this little girl. After I fed and changed Alexis, I put her to sleep. I took a shower and then relaxed. My phone was ringing off the hook. Carmen called me from Miami. We talked about the baby and the delivery. I told her that I'm enjoying motherhood even though it's only been a couple of days. She asked if I had written to Michael. I told her not yet. As a matter of fact, I said, when I hang up from you, I will start writing the letter just as Dr. Palmer suggested to me. Let me get off of this phone, Denise. My bill is high enough. Ok, I'll talk to you soon. Love you. Bye.

After the baby woke up, I changed her, fed her and held her some more. She is so cute and so soft, I said to myself. Alexis was definitely worth the while. All that I have gone through with Michael and this pregnancy didn't really bother me too much now. Once Alexis dozed off again, I started writing Michael. The letter went like this:

Dear Michael:

I am writing to tell you that I had the baby. It's a girl. Her name is Alexis Reneé . I know the reason why you lied to me; it's because you were getting married. It's a damn shame you tried to get me to have an abortion for this reason. Your lies and deceptions definitely caught up with you. But, I am not going to dwell on that. What's happened, happened. The baby is here now. All I want to know is if you want to be a part of this baby's life or not. I would have liked to have put a picture of Alexis in the envelope for you, but I felt that you may not look at it. If you want to talk to me about this situation, please give me a call. My new phone number is 555-5153. If I don't hear from you, I'll just assume you're really not interested.

Sincerely,

Denise

The next day when I went to apply for the baby's social security number. Then I went to the post office to mail the letter to Michael, certified. I wonder what the outcome is going to be. Will he read the letter or will he just throw it away once he knows its from me? These were some of the questions that crossed my mind.

On Friday, the thirteenth of all days, I got a phone call. When I answered the phone, it was Michael. I was shocked. I didn't know what to say or how to react. Denise, this is Michael. Yeah. Why are you acting so sarcastic, he asked? Excuse me, I said. Anyway, I got your letter. Ok. Will you be home this evening? Yes I will. Alone, he said? Yes, alone. Why, what difference does it make? What's your address? It's 310 Huckleberry Lane, #14. See you then. Bye. Click.

When bell rung about eight o'clock, all I could think of was the last time Michael came over my house. I buzzed him in. My heart was pounding. I went to pick the baby up from her crib. I opened the door and there Michael was. He came in. I offered him to have a seat. Neither one of us said anything at first. Then he finally had the nerve to ask me what was up as if nothing has ever happened. A sick dude.

I started asking Michael why he did what he did to me even though I really know the truth now. And he responded by saying, "he didn't know." What do you mean you don't know, I asked? I know you are married and all but I need to know one thing: "Are you are going to be a part of Alexis' life or not now that she is in this world?" Either you're going to be in it or not. Michael said that he wanted to be in his daughter's life and that he wanted to see her a lot. We agreed to a schedule.

Chapter 10

As time went on our relationship grew into a deep friendship. It was pretty good, considering everything that had happened. We laughed. Michael gave me birthday gifts, Mother's Day gifts, Christmas gifts and we even went on a couple of vacations together.

One thing led to another. We started sleeping together again. This time it was different. As our feelings started getting deeper and deeper, the pressure was on. Michael started telling me how much he loves me and he wants to be with me and Alexis. I began to love Michael and wanted us to be a family also. As time went on, the situation was becoming too difficult. I wanted more. I wanted to be on a different level with him. I couldn't deal with Michael coming over at his convenience. I would call him at work and he would say he's coming, then he'll call back and tell me he couldn't come because something came up. I would get highly upset everytime. This isn't going to work, I thought.

I had come to realize that Michael started lying again and playing games with me again. One time we had an argument about his wife, Karen. I couldn't understand if Michael was so unhappy and felt that he had made a mistake by getting married to her, then why couldn't he just get out of it? What's the problem? Michael would tell me he's working on it. His wife was a woman who portrayed to be all that, but didn't have a damn thing. She couldn't stand me as if it was all of my fault. But the feelings were mutual – I couldn't stand her project bitch ass either.

One time I called Karen on her job. I asked her if Michael had told her the truth about everything and she said she would rather not say. Then I mentioned to her that Michael said he wanted to have overnight visits with Alexis and I wanted to know how she felt about it. This heffer went off by saying, "look bitch, that's between you and Michael." "I don't want anything to do with this situation." I asked her if she meant she didn't want anything to do with the situation or Alexis to clarify. "Do you know this project chick had a nerve to say yes to both?" Right then and there I realized that she didn't give a damn and that she's very angry about this situation and wasn't going to deal with it either. She wanted no parts of it. Karen was definitely not trying to play step-mommy to Alexis. In a way, I couldn't blame her because she was deceived and lied to as well. But that wasn't my fault. It was Michael's fault and she needs to deal with him on that and take it out on him.

The next day Michael called going off about me calling Karen. I told him I needed to know how his wife felt about Alexis before I let him keep her overnight. A big argument broke out. We didn't speak for a month or so.

After we started speaking again, Michael told me that he was leaving his wife. I felt kind of was happy, but not completely happy. To me, it did not feel right. Finally, I thought we would be together. Michael started coming over and staying longer than usual. I love you, he said. Things are going to work out. I asked him if he had filed for divorce and he said not yet. I didn't pressure him. After we had dinner and Alexis was sound asleep, we made love. The one thing that pissed me off was when Michael and I would sleep together, we never talked. He always got up to leave. When he's gone, I felt depressed and lonely. Ugh, that was a bad feeling I felt. This isn't right.

I called Michael at work and was told that he was on vacation all week. I was confused. All kinds of things were flowing through my mind. I decided to call his wife's job out of curiosity. When I called, the receptionist said "I'm sorry, but Karen's on vacation this week." I felt a big lump in my throat and my eyes began to fill with tears. I was hurt and very confused. If Michael is planning on getting a divorce, why in the hell would he and his wife be on vacation together? At the same time? Same week? I told myself to get real, to wake up and to look at the big picture. Stupid.

The following week when Michael returned to work, I called him. I questioned him about his vacation. He tried to tell me that he went on vacation by himself. You know I did not go for that bullshit. Are you kidding me? Michael asked if he can come over that evening to see me and then we could talk. I agreed because I had a lot to say and a lot to get off of my chest. Of course when Michael came, he did his song and dance and said all the right things to me. I wasn't mad at him any longer. We made love, then he left. Ugh, I'm a damn fool! Once again, I felt like El Cheapo.

The lies continued. There was another time when Michael told me that he was leaving his wife again and he needed money to get a place. I found out that he and his wife moved into another apartment complex. Another time Michael asked me if he could borrow a large sum of money from me. When I asked him for what, he said he needed it to make some kind of investment. Shortly after that, he had pulled up in a brand new Lexus. I was shocked and I had asked Michael did he use the money I loaned him to get the car. He had the nerve to say yes. I asked that dog bitch why couldn't he ask his wife for the money. It's two of you and one of me. "Denise, it's not like I'm not paying you back. You will have all of your money next week when I get paid." "That's not the point," I said. "Take your ass on and go to hell Michael," I shouted! He tried to explain but I didn't listen. Of course the lies continued and continued. This is just a hot mess.

One thing I didn't quite understand: Did Michael's family even know about his daughter? I used to ask Michael if he would take Alexis with him when he goes to visit his mother. He never did. I remember when Michael's mother came to visit him, he didn't even bring his mom by to meet or to see his daughter. No one in his family never called. That only told me that they knew nothing about Alexis. Either that or they didn't want to get involved since he was married. But hey, that wasn't my fucking fault. He lied and when I found out, I was already caught up. Dumb motherfuckers! They are all ignorant to me. One other time, Michael and I went on a vacation. He gave me a postcard to put in the mailbox that was addressed to his mother. I wrote down her address. When we returned from vacation, I decided to write her. I told her all about Alexis. I also included my return address and phone number. Shockingly, I never heard a word from his mom. Who do I blame, her or Michael, I asked myself? You know what? I blame Michael's simple ass. He should have been honest and up front about everything in the beginning. I know Alexis is in the dark where his family is concerned. I can feel it.

Things got worse and worse between us. I lived not too far from Michael and his wife. You would think Michael would help me out in some kind of way, but he didn't. One thing he was sure of, was that he wasn't letting me get too close to the home front. It was like we were living this big lie. Noone knew about us. It was only between me and him. I remember when there was a snow storm and I had to shovel six inches of snow from around my car before I could even take Alexis to the daycare. I was burning up mad. I was heated. When I got to work, I called Michael and blasted him. I told him that he could have at least called me this morning to see if I needed any kind of help. Michael responded by saying, "I had to shovel my own car out." Dang, that's cold. I said, well you at least could have taken Alexis to the daycare. Michael showed no sympathy and actually thought this was funny. I just shook my head in disgust.

I had to do everything. When Alexis was sick, I had to stay home or if she was at daycare, I had to leave early to pick her up. I would ask Michael if he could leave early but there was always an excuse. Michael had excuses for everything. When I wanted him to come over, he had stuff to do after work. When I needed him to pick up Alexis from daycare, he had a late meeting. What the fuck was he good for? Actually, nothing but lies, games and more bullshit.

Suddenly, I came to realize that Michael was still the same and was bullshitting me around. He didn't care about me. It was all about him having a wife for keeps and something on the side for play time. Everytime I wanted to break it off with Michael, he didn't want to or acted like he didn't want to or would ask me a stupid question like, "why?" Why? Are you kidding me? I couldn't deal with this any longer. This is an unhealthy situation, I told myself.

First of all, Michael doesn't respect me. Nevertheless, he doesn't even spend time with Alexis. My girlfriend Marcy always told me that he doesn't care about me or Alexis. I thought he at least would care about Alexis, if not me. All Michael cared about was his own happiness and what he wanted. Fuck what I wanted or needed. My wants and needs were irrelevant to him. He didn't take my feelings into consideration at all. I need to make a permanent decision about this situation once and for all.

The thing that bothered me the most, was that his family didn't even have anything to do with Alexis. I never understood this. I realized that I was definitely getting out of this situation for good. That's when I decided to move to Atlanta. To hell with Michael, his wife, his family and definitely his bullshit. I'm out of here!

Chapter 11

I moved to Atlanta the Summer of 1991 with Alexis. I rented a two bedroom apartment that was off the hook for only four hundred and twenty five dollars a month. I was living large compared to where I was living up north. An apartment up north would cost way over nine hundred dollars a month to rent.

I didn't know a soul in suburban Atlanta. I had family in Atlanta but not on the side I was living on. I figured once I started working, I would meet people. It felt great moving to another town where no one knew me. This was definitely the chance to start over fresh. I left Michael and all of his bullshit behind and up north. Although, he told me that he was leaving his wife and moving to Alabama, that did not phase me one bit and most importantly, it was not my problem. I didn't believe him, neither did I care. I was like "work it out." "Not my problem!" "Good luck," I told him. I was done.

Two weeks later Michael called me in Atlanta to tell me that he quit his job at the bank and that he was leaving for Alabama, but first he was coming to Atlanta. I told Michael in a blunt expression, "you're not coming to where I am." I can't tell you not to come to Atlanta, but

I can tell you not to come to my house. I left from up there to start fresh and to meet new people. After our conversation was over and all of the drama that followed the conversation, I agreed to let Michael stop through on his way down to Alabama, to at least see Alexis. This would be the last time I see Michael or deal with him. I was 100% through with his ass. If Michael decided not to ever see Alexis after this, that would be fine with me. Life goes on.

When Michael got to Atlanta, he called. I gave him directions to my house. Shortly I got a knock on my door. I knew it would be Michael. Afterall, who did I know on this side of Atlanta that would be knocking at my door? I opened the door and let him in. We had small talk. I was kind of sympathetic and don't know why, but since he had a ways to go and had been driving all night long, I decided that he could sleep over and leave FIRST in the morning. He slept on the sofa.

Two days later, Michael was still at my house. The good thing was that nothing happened between the two of us. I was totally fed up with Michael, his lies and all of his bullshit. I didn't want anything else to do with him except where it concerned Alexis. He told me that he would be leaving later this evening and asked me if that is alright with me. I had no problem with it since the evening was only a few hours away. Thank you Jesus, I said to myself. I didn't have a car at the time, so I had Michael take me to the grocery store before he left. When we got back to the apartment, I cooked dinner for us.

After we ate, we talked some more. Micahel took a shower, pack the few things he had taken out and put them in his duffle bag. As Michael headed out the door and starting walking towards his car, we hugged and said our goodbyes. Whew, weight was just lifted off of my shoulders. I'm so rid of him. I had no more feelings for Michael. He is history in my book. Yes!!

Chapter 12

I decided to take out the trash. Damn, it was too hot. I had on a spandex top that showed my stomach and spandex shorts. On my way walking back to my house, there were these guys standing around. One of them yelled, "hey babe, how are you doing today?" I said, fine. I can cleary see that. Do you have a minute? I really wanted to say no, but I didn't. I rolled my eyes in my head as he was walking towards me. As he was getting closer to me, I said to myself, damn he's fine! What's your name, he asked? Denise. Hi Denise, I'm Jamal. Hey. You live around here? Yeah. Jamal told me how good I looked. I smiled. Really, he said. I thanked him for the compliment. At that point, Jamal broke out and said, "oh baby you look so sweet and sexy with that mole on the side of your back." I couldn't help laughing at his southern Atlanta accent.

I could tell Jamal was cool. When he asked me which building I lived in, I told him a different one other than the actual one. Afterall, I was living on the east side of Atlanta by myself and I wasn't trusting a damn soul. Shit, he could be the Atlanta strangler for all I know. I wasn't taking any chances.

After we chatted for a while, we exchanged phone numbers. I preferred talking to him on the phone rather than face-to-face; at least until I felt comfortable. But as time went on, our conversations grew and I got to that comfort level with Jamal. That's when I invited him over. God, was he handsome! I could tell Jamal was attracted to me. We definitely clicked with each other. I realized that I was finally getting some relief of happiness. Michael was slowly but surely getting out of my system. I definitely made the right move to Atlanta. H-O-T-L-A-N-T-A, here I am! Get ready because a new sister is in town.

Just when things seem to be going so good, there is always a monkey wrench being thrown into the game. One day Jamal told me that he was attracted to me and was interested in seeing me. But first, he said he needed to tell me something about his past that I should know before anyone in the neighborhood would have the chance to tell me. I asked him, what is it? I had one eyebrow raised and was looking at Jamal puzzled.

What I'm about to tell you Denise is that at one point in my life, I used to sell drugs. I had houses, cars and even put an old girlfriend of mine through college. What happened next, I asked? I got busted and went to the penitentiary, you know jail as in locked up. The Feds. I'm like ok, so what's up? Oh nothing is up now. I paid my dues for what I did. I'm straight now. I just wanted you to know this about me. But I can understand and respect you if you decide not to deal with me after what I just told you. When I thought about what Jamal said, it really didn't matter to me because for one it was before my time and since he has paid his debt to society and everything is straight, then I'm cool with it. I made my decision right then and there that I wanted to continue seeing Jamal, as a friend. At least he was upfront with me from the very beginning about his legal past and problems. People do change and can change for the better, I told myself. Ha, what a joke! Life begins with Jamal – but just for a short, hot moment though.

Chapter 13

My relationship with Jamal was cool to me. Our feelings were mutual. We went for walks and communicated about everything you can think of. There was one thing about Jamal I found out is that he too, is a liar and seemed to be a playboy. Oh and not to mention, lazy. The next thing I knew, Jamal started telling me he had to call me back and never did. One day I was trying to locate him. I was blowing his cell phone up, I went to his house and I asked people in the neighborhood if they had seen him. I didn't hear from Jamal for about a good week or so. When I finally caught up with him, I asked him, "where have you been?" He had the nerve to tell me he went to Miami. Why did you go to Miami? To work, he answered. You mean to tell me you left Atlanta to go to Miami to work for a whole week? Yep, he replied. What happened to your job here? Did you get fired or laid off? No, I did not. Jamal was lying. Let me ask you something, Jamal. How come you couldn't call me from Miami? Because I was too busy to call. Too busy doing what, may I ask? Working Denise, damn! I looked at him like he was fucking crazy. You're lying Jamal. Just admit it. I think you went to Miami to sell drugs. You must be getting back into that world. He denied every word. But I knew better.

At times I would get on Jamal about getting a real job making honest money. He always had some kind of line to feed me. Bottom line: The brother did not want to work or at least not work on some white man's job. That is Jamal's copout for not wanting to work a legit job. He wanted to call his own shots. How can you call your own shots with no formal education behind you and no job experience of any sort? Sounds crazy and idiotic to me. Jamal must really think I am stupid. One thing I knew for sure was that I wanted a man with a decent job and stable income. I have never associated myself with men who laid around or hung out with his friends in the "hood" all damn day long doing nothing. We would get into arguments about this all the time. I always told Jamal we would not last long if he didn't get his act together. Jamal bullshitted a lot also.

I told Jamal if he wanted us to at least try to be together, he had to be more responsible. Plain and simple. I was dead set against taking care of a grown ass man. We need to be fifty fifty with what we were doing. I wasn't having it any other way – a different story.

One time Jamal told me I talked too much. I put him in his place quick. I let him know that I will always speak my mind. You think I'm going to let you control my domain and my destiny, I asked? I don't think so brother. For one, you are not my man. I don't know the type of women you had in your past Jamal, but I'm here to tell you, I'm not the one who can be told just anything and fall for it. I don't go for no man trying to have control over me and telling me what to do, what to think, what to say and when to say it. I've been down that road before. Shut up Denise, Jamal yelled! No, you shut up! Let me tell you something Jamal, you need to bounce if you think you are going to control everything. You're tripping girl. I know what you need Denise.

Then he starts laughing. Jamal looked at me with a peace sign along with a slanted smile on his face. We both started laughing. I could never stay mad a Jamal for a long time. He was also funny.

But for real, I'm serious Jamal. If you can't deal, leave me alone. He looked at me and said, "you think you're bad, don't you?" No I don't. It's just that I'm in control of who I am and what I do.

I told Jamal I had to go because I have a meeting first thing in the morning at work.

When I arrived at Citizens and Southern Bank, I took the elevator up to the 7th floor where I worked. I put my belongings up and headed towards the conference room.

It was announced by the department head that we will be getting laid off the following week. I panicked. What will I do? I have no backup plan. The job market was extremely slow due to the recession. There were no jobs out there. None, not even temporary work.

Every Sunday, I bought the Atlanta Journal Constitution newspaper. I searched and checked off jobs that interested me. I sent resumés out like crazy to various companies. I got no responses from not one of them. None, zero!

The following week, I was laid off. As time went on, I had no luck finding another job. My money was running short and I decided that I would have to go back north. I had to make this decision to go back north because one thing I knew for sure, Jamal wasn't a man that I could depend on and he was definitely irresponsible. I could not take the chance either with Jamal. He would let me down. I made up my mind that I will have to go back for a little bit or just until the economy gets better. I was getting stressed about this. I definitely did not want to leave Atlanta. I felt as though I was going backwards instead of forward. I had come such a long way.

I called Jamal and told him I needed to talk to him. When he arrived, I filled him in on the scoop. I'll be leaving Atlanta to go back home. Jamal got upset. I told him I couldn't afford to stay in Atlanta with no job, a child to support, rent to be paid and with no health insurance. "You and Alexis can move in with me," he said. "Really, I'm serious." "Are you kidding me Jamal?" "You have no place of your own." "You are so full of shit and it stinks." "Besides, you're not stable yourself." "You're right." "Denise is always right." "That's right man, you know it." I chuckled. When are you going to leave? In a couple of days. Jamal looked so sad. I really liked Jamal a lot and he told me one day I was going to be his wife. I ignored that completely. Not. I knew this was never going to happen. "This brother is about a bunch of bullshit." I did not like Jamal in that way. I would never marry someone like Jamal. He's too unstable for me. He is cool but weak as a man. He can't hold it down. I promised him we would definitely keep in touch with each other.

The day I left Atlanta, I was boo hooing like a baby. I didn't get a chance to say goodbye to Jamal. I never heard from him since the day I told him I was heading back north. Did he forget I was leaving? Jamal always pulled disappearing acts from time to time. This is a routine act for him so I am not surprised at all. The bottom line with Jamal is that he was useless to me and he was below my standards. But because of his down-to-earth southern personality and coolness, I fell for him but only in a friendship way. I was trying to keep my mind off of Michael and Jamal came along at the right time. Afterall, I did not know anyone else besides him. It was fun while it lasted. I will always be Jamal's friend though.

We took Amtrak back north. It seemed like I cried all the way. Going back home just made me depressed because I left all the bad memories there. I prayed to God he will see me through and show me the way.

One thing I was sure about, when I see my way clear again, I'll be back to Atlanta. That was a one hundred percent guarantee. Not only did I feel bad about leaving Atlanta, but I felt I was leaving my plans and dreams behind as well.

As far as Jamal playing a major role in my life, that was out of the question. It wasn't even an option. He is not man enough for me. I decided not to look back where Jamal is concerned. I cut him out of my life for the time being. No hard feelings.

Chapter 14

It's been two years now that I have been back from Atlanta. I was still stressed over the fact of being back in the north. My plan is to focus on me and Alexis for now and my longterm plans for us. My every intentions were to get back to Atlanta as soon as possible.

I decided to go visit with my mother. The neighbors that lived downstairs were planning a surprise birthday cookout for their mother, who is suffering from Alzheimer's disease. My mother was invited and asked me to come with her. At first, I refused. But then I thought, what the heck. I had nothing else on my agenda to do.

At the cookout, I smelled the works that are always being grilled at a barbeque. The smoke was really smoking. They had the works! You hear me? People were scattered all around the yard. The music was pumping loud. Some people were dancing, popping their fingers and bouncing their heads to the music.

Shelley, who is Mrs. Anderson's daughter, came over to us and told us to get something to eat. We got up and went to get our grub on. I had a plate with collard greens, potatoe salad, barbecue ribs and a cold pepsi. I sat down where I was originally sitting. My mother and Alexis

72

were right behind me. I started talking to my mother about teens and how a lot of them are either dropping out of school, selling drugs or using drugs.

Across from us sat this tall, brown skinned handsome guy. He heard our conversation and conveniently joined in. No one asked him his opinion. LOL! By the way, my name is Eddie. Hi, I'm Denise. This is my mother and my daughter, Alexis. "Good to meet you all," he said. I smiled and said likewise.

Eddie started asking us who we knew. The Anderson's are neighbors of mine, my mom replied. Oh ok, Eddie replied. My two sons are over there in the shade sitting under the tree. Eddie pointed to his sons. What, I said! Those two boys are your sons? Oh my goodness, what a small world? I have known Kenny and Greg since they were little boys. What, Eddie asked? Yep. Kenny used to go to the private school my sister Tameka goes to now.

Tameka's your sister, Eddie asked? She sure is. Wow, it is a small world, isn't it? Eddie smiled and shook his head. Unbelievable!

Eddie was checking me out left and right. He kept talking to me; going on and on. I wondered if he was ever going to shut up. I chuckled to myself.

"So Denise, where do you live," Eddie asked? "I live on the south side." "Really?" "So do I," Eddie said. "Wow!" "That's interesting," I replied. "I'm surprised I have never bumped into you." "I drive the public bus out that way." "Oh really and I take the public bus out that way." We both cracked up in laughter. "Well, it's getting late and I need to get going," Eddie said. Eddie called Kenny and Greg over and told them they were about to leave. I spoke to the boys, gave them a hug and asked them if they remember me. They did vaguely. Well it was such a pleasure talking to you Denise. Yeah, good talking to you too.

A month had passed since meeting Eddie. I still had not bumped into him in passing in the town we lived in. Maybe our timing is off or something. I really didn't know anyone in this lily white neighborhood and was hoping we bumped heads.

The next day I went to the salon to get a relaxer and a cut. I started wearing my hair cut really short. It was sharp. I called my mother from the salon and told her that I'll be over when I'm done and after I pick up a few groceries from the supermarket.

It was such a big treat for me to go the Jamaican-West Indian tropical supermarket because the prices were much cheaper than the bigger supermarkets. The Jamacian-West Indian supermarkets were only in the black neighborhoods. I lived in a lily white town, where they act like they have never heard of grits before. They did not even have collard greens in the grocery stores out there. I had to go in the hood to get my stuff. At the tropical supermarket, I could spend thirty five dollars for groceries and come out with five to seven bags of food. That's how dirt cheap the prices were and the prices defintiely worked for me and my pocket book. That was too funny.

As I pulled into my mother's parking lot, I realized the tall, handsome guy talking to my mom, was Eddie. I said to myself, oh my goodness, there's that guy from the cookout. I parked my car and got out of my car. I went over to say hello to my mom and Eddie. That's a sharp haircut Denise, Eddie complimented. Thank you, thank you. I like it myself, I must say. I smiled. My mother heard her phone ringing and went upstairs to catch it before it could stop ringing. Eddie and I started talking as if we've known each other for a long time. He was showing me the inside of his brand new car, then he told me that he and his sons drove down to Atlanta to their family reunion. Oh really, I said. I used to live there. What? Yes sir, indeed I did. We laughed. Eddie asked me which route I take when I go down. "I go I95 south to I85 south." He pulled his map out and showed me the way he went. I started laughing. "What's so funny," he asked? "You went the long way." "I did," he asked amusingly? We both cracked up.

Eddie was about to leave. He gave me his phone number and his address. Dang, he moves fast! He asked me to call him so we can get together and throw some steaks on the grill. I said cool.

I called my girlfriend Linda and told her all about Eddie. "Sounds interesting," Linda said. He is and I like him, as a friend and someone to chat with. "I need a good friend in my life with a sense of humor." "Someone I can talk to, hang out with and just go with the flow of everyday life." "I don't want any strings attached." "I just want to be friends with a guy at this point." There is nothing wrong with that Denise. After my last two relationships, I need a breather. I was so mentally drained, especially with Michael and his bullshit. Jamal was someone to just kick it around with until something comes along better. I don't want another man at this time. I want to be free and do me and Alexis at this time. I need to get myself together and to regroup. "I hate being back up here." "It's only temporary Denise." "I know it is Linda," I replied.

One evening my daughter Alexis was at my mother's for the evening. I wanted some company. So I decided that I'll give Eddie a call. Oh fuck, I couldn't even find his phone number, so I ended up spending the evening reading and watching tv. All alone. Another time. When I came home from work, Eddie gave me a call. I told him I had to get back to him. For some reason, every time Eddie called me, he caught me at the wrong time. I never got the chance to call him back.

I picked Alexis up from daycare and took her to my mother's again. I wanted to do some good old fashion house cleaning for the weekend. When I got home, I warmed up some leftover Chinese food. Damn it was good.

I started cleaning. When I looked under the kitchen table, I saw a small white piece of paper sticking out. I picked it up, looked at it and there it was right in front of my eyes - Eddie's name, address and phone number. When I finished cleaning, I gave Eddie a call. I was happy I found his number.

The phone ranged. "Hello," the sexy voice answered. "Hi Eddie, this is Denise." "Well, well, well, look who's calling?" I laughed. "I can't believe you finally called me!" "I wanted to call much sooner, but I misplaced your number." We chatted for a while. Eddie is definitely cool and can hold down a good conversation. He's someone who I can relate to.

The next evening, Eddie invited us over to have dinner with him and his son Greg. Eddie cooked an excellent meal with side salads and made punch to drink.

Eddie blessed the food. At the dinner table, we cracked silly jokes. "Eddie, you are a good cook." "Your food is very tasty." "Thanks Denise." "You're welcome." After dinner, I washed and dried the dishes. An hour later, Alexis and I were back home. Eddie called to make sure we got there safely.

After I put Alexis to bed, I called Eddie back. I loved talking with him and I liked him in my presence. "Denise," Eddie said, "I really enjoyed you and your daughter this evening." "And if you don't mind, I would like to start seeing more of you if that's alright with you?" "Yes, it is alright with me," I answered. We talked a little longer, then said goodnight to each other.

Chapter 15

After three months of hanging out with Eddie, we started dating. We both came to the conclusion that we were falling in love with one another. We had so much in common. Eddie and I hadn't had an intimate relationship at this point. I started going to church on a regular basis and wanted to do things in a godly manner. Eddie didn't pressure me about making love at first. I knew I had a prince charming and a very respectful man. Eddie was loving to me and very kind. He treated my like a queen. He cooked for me and every morning he would call me just to tell me how beautiful I am and how much he loves me. He was sweet.

Eventually, Eddie started putting the pressure on me about making love. We would have arguments about it. I explained to Eddie that I wanted a stronger relationship with God, I wanted to get baptized and I would feel guilty if I indulged in sex. Denise, a man has to know what that's all about and what he is getting before he jumps into a marriage. A marriage, I questioned? We are not getting married no time soon. Put it this way Denise, it's like testing the waters. You can have everything going good in the relationship, but if the love making part of it isn't there, one or the other will stray away. I told Eddie to have some faith. He couldn't see eye-to-eye with me on this situation.

Finally I gave in. After that happened, we made love constantly. It was nonstop – morning, noon and night. It bothered me because I continued to go to church every Sunday along with Alexis. I felt like a hypocrit. Also, Eddie and Greg started attending church services with us.

We had a strong relationship. Eddie called me every single morning when he came home on his break from work. We would always talk for about an half hour.

Eddie came to Alexis' school plays, taught her how to ride her bike and accepted her as his own daughter. Eddie would give me massages from head-to-toe, breakfast in bed and when he was on vacation, he would take me to and from work. Alexis and I would stay over Eddie's house, which he owned. On school nights we would have Alexis and Greg in bed by nine o'clock. In the morning, I would get the kids up, make breakfast for them and pack their snacks for school. Most of the time, Kenny would leave very early in the morning for school with his homeboys in one of those old school cars with the big rims. I believe it is a Chevy Caprice.

Eddie also had a third son named James. Another baby mama! Kenny and Greg were from Shelley, who is Eddie's ex-wife and also my mother's neighbor's daughter. Eddie had temporary custody of the boys from Shelley because she was strung out on drugs badly, would leave the kids in the home alone and often left them with no food in the house for them to eat. Damn, at least have food for your kids in the house. To top it off, the Department of Social Services were threatening to take them from her and put them in a foster home. It became a bad situation. Eventually Eddie got legal custody of Kenny and Greg. Shelley was upset but Eddie had to take matters into his own hands. He was looking out for the benefit of the kids, not for her benefit. Shelley knew once the kids were out of her possession all of her government assistance would stop. Shit, by law she is required to pay Eddie child support. But with no job, how could she?

Eddie and Shelley didn't get along for nothing in the world. Shelley would call and Eddie would start going off. There was always a big argument between them. I couldn't understand it. Eddie would call Shelley a no good mother, who doesn't even take care of her own kids and she would call Eddie a punk and tell him someone needed to kick his ass. I never understood why they were always at each other's throats. I stayed out of that drama between them. It wasn't my place anyway to get into that.

When Eddie married Shelley, he owned a six family unit house. Eddie told me how family members in his family and Shelley's family were pressuring him about putting her name on the mortgage note. I asked Eddie why was he reluctant to do so. He said he just wanted to wait for a while. Sooner or later, Shelley's name was added to Eddie's mortgage note.

Eddie claims when he added Shelley's name to the mortgage note, she changed. That's when all hell broke loose. He said there was a time he wanted them to move south to get Shelley away from the drug scene and their families. But Shelley refused. Eddie said Shelley would be so high and that she would go completely off when mentioning moving away. What did she say, I asked? Shelley said to me, "I'm not moving no fucking where." Whoa! Those are strong words. Tell me about it.

Later on down the line through all of the drama with the marriage, Shelley became pregnant again. Eddie said the pregnancy was a difficult one and that Shelley had delivered a baby girl, but the baby did not make it. Oh no, poor little thing. May god rest her soul. I asked Eddie what was the problem? You know, Denise, I believe Shelley wanted to have a miscarriage because she was still dipping and dabbing with the drugs and she probably wasn't sure if the baby was mine or not. She was all over the place.

But when my baby girl was born, she looked just like me. A year later Greg was born. Wow, I said.

Two years later they were divorced. Eddie said his marriage had ended in a nasty divorce. The divorce took over three years to get resolved because Shelley wanted eighty five percent of the proceeds. With all the fighting and carrying on with the divorce, they both ended up with three thousand dollars. Out of one hundred thousand dollars and with all of the litigation costs, it boiled down to three thousand dollars a piece. That's a damn shame. And for what? Greed.

I was definitely interested in everything Eddie had to say. I needed to know what I was getting into. Afterall, there are two sides to every story and this was Eddie's. I never heard Shelley's. I asked Eddie to tell me about Pam, who is his youngest son James' mother. He said they didn't get along either. I was amazed. What the hell? What's up with that?

When I met Eddie, he had been broken up with Pam eighteen months ago. The two were back and forth in court over child support payments. According to Eddie, Pam was greedy for money and she flipped out when she found out he had bought and paid cash for a brand new car, then turned around and bought a townhouse.

Pam called Eddie constantly. I questioned Eddie why she called so much. It seemed like the same or similar problems that had occurred with Shelley. "Denise, Pam has a serious problem, she's crazy and doesn't understand that it's over." "After eighteen months," I asked? Yep, Eddie responded. I was like, strange. Something did not seem right but I went along with what he was telling me.

In my heart, I felt there was more to Eddie and Pam. For some reason, the two of them were constantly at each other's throat. But, why was the question? If it's over, it's over. Especially after eighteen months.

Another time Eddie and I were having a deep conversation about Pam. He told me Pam threw a huge rock at his window. When the rock came crashing through the window it almost hit Greg in the head. He also said the reason why he and Pam were in and out of court is because when they were at a previous hearing, they had an argument and in the middle of the argument, Pam blurted out, "I don't know why you want to take care of James anyway, because he's not even your son." When I heard this Denise, I was shocked and I fucking freaked out. Before we left the court, I had my attorney file a motion for a paternity test. A couple of weeks later, Pam was notified.

When the day came to go to court on this hearing, she didn't show up. The judge ordered Pam to court and if she did a no show, a warrant would be put out for her arrest. A couple of weeks later, the three of us were at the lab having a paternity test done. The lab tech told us it would take between 3 to 6 weeks for the results. Ok, so let me me ask you something Eddie? You were married to Pam as well? No, I wasn't. I was frowning and blowing out air. This is a trip, I said. What's the problem, Denise? I guess I am just shocked. Don't worry about it. So we get the paternity test back from the lab. It's declared that I am James' dad. I knew I was but it was one of Pam's tactics to hold onto me. Crazy, I thought.

I thought to myself, isn't this a red flag for me not to be in this relationship? Too much went on with Eddie and his past two relationships. The first with his ex-wife, the second with his second baby mama. Eddie was good to me though. His past relationships were complicated and confusing to me. Why would such a nice guy, have so many women problems? Was it something he wasn't doing right? What was it with him? I wondered.

Eddie could talk. I was so tired of hearing about Shelley and Pam. I guess Eddie got going on the subject. All of a sudden, Eddie was telling me how he and Shelley met.

In the beginning they were friends. Apparently, Shelley had been in an abusive relationship with her brothers. Shelley confided in Eddie about her problems.

One thing led to another. They started seeing each other more and more. Eddie used to smoke and sell weed, had California curls and was living the fast life. Shelley, at the time, was a good girl. She saw how Eddie was living and asked him if he wanted her to go out and sell her body for him, so he claims. Hell no, Eddie told her! You are my main woman. He said the subject never came up again.

During the time Eddie was seeing Shelley, he was also seeing some-one name Kim. He told me Kim was his first love from the past and before he even met Shelley. She was respectful, honest and she was the first woman he took the time with to learn about a woman's body.

Why did you and Kim break up, I asked? I started seeing Kim again at the same time I was seeing Shelley and they both found out. So in other words, you were sleeping with both of them and feeding them the same bullshit lines. That's about the size of it Denise, Eddie said. That's not right. I know, but I did it. So heartless. Seems like you were a dog to me. Don't trip Denise. Whatever!

You know what Denise? One day Kim was at my house, right. She ended up spending the entire evening with me. Shelley had been there two nights ago. Go on, I'm listening, with raised eyebrows. Anyway, Kim told me she had a feeling I was seeing someone else. And I was, but naturally I lied. She had her doubts though. No good, no good. I was shaking my head. "Go on, I said."

I decided to take a shower and when I got out, Kim was at the door holding a silk night gown and silk panties, and asked me what's up with this shit? At that moment, I knew I was busted. That's when I told her the truth about Shelley.

To make a long story short, Kim broke it off. She told me she was moving back to Jacksonville. We kept in touch for a while. Our relationship finally came to an end. I went to visit her to try to rekindle our relationship. When I got to Jacksonville, I got a big surprise. I found out Kim had moved on with her life and she was married. I got on the next flight heading back north. I was crushed and so hurt. Well Eddie you know what goes around comes around. True that. I deserved it. I'll say.

When I returned home from Jacksonville, Shelley told me she was pregnant. Nine months later, my oldest son Kenny was born. We got married and the rest is history.

Wow, you sure had your share of problems and issues with these women! You know something Denise, you're the first woman I have really and truly loved. I have never loved anyone like I love you. I responded to Eddie by telling him that I am not sure about that one, but ok if you say so. For some reason, I had a problem believing that. Again, I went along with it.

Chapter 16

*E*ddie asked me to marry him. I accepted. I was so excited. I was younger than Eddie and I felt that he could take me places I have never been, give me experiences I have never encountered and he could show and teach me new things. We planned for the wedding to take place in the fall. I was happy and so was Eddie (or so it seemed). Eddie and I always did things together and with the kids. We took them to church, the movies, out to eat and barbequed with them. It was great. Everyone got along really well and there were no conflicts.

We decided to wait until we get married before living together. I moved into a one bedroom apartment with Alexis to save some money. While we were taking a break from moving, Eddie and I sat on his bed. Whew, I'm exhausted. Me too Eddie. I need to get me some ice cold water. I was sweating and all. Eddie looked at me like he wanted to tell me something. "What's up," I asked? I had a funny feeling. I have to get something off my chest Denise. Ok, like what, I asked? Listen to me. Ok. Do you know that Pam and I were married? "What," married? Yeah, right Eddie. You really are tripping. For real, I'm serious. I looked at Eddie's facial expression and realized that he was dead serious. Now,

I am really confused. I thought I asked you if you and Pam were ever married and you told me no. Stop playing with me Eddie. Don't play like that. Eddie was still looking at me very seriously and said, no joke. I sighed, rolled my eyes and blew out some air. You can ask Kenny. I immediately backed up from Eddie. Ok, I will go ask Kenny and if he tells me some bullshit about you being married to Pam, then it is over. I could feel I was about to start tripping. I could feel it in my heart. Kenny had his room door was closed. I knocked on the door. Kenny opened the door. Hey Kenny, I need to ask you something. Ok, he said. Was your father ever married to Pam? Yes. Are you sure? Yeah, they were. Alright. Is everything ok Kenney asked? Yeah, everything is fine. Don't' worry about it. I walked out of Kenney's room feeling so confused, betrayed and hurt. I pushed, no kicked Eddie's door open and went totally off. Nigger, you lied to me! You lied to me! You deceived me! You are a big liar, manipulator and a cheat! I asked you a long time ago if you and Pam were ever married. And what did you tell me? You told me no. Denise, calm down please! Don't put your fucking hands on me. Get the fuck away from me! Listen Denise, the reason why I kept it from you is because I didn't want to lose you. I knew if I told you that I was in the middle of divorcing Pam, which in fact was about to be finalized, you wouldn't have been with me. You damn right, I wouldn't have! So you decided to make the decision for me, huh? Oh wait a minute, hold up! So when you met me you were still legally married to Pam, right? Right. What the fuck? Are you crazy Eddie? You deceived me. I can't deal with this. You are a selfish bastard and wasn't thinking of my feelings, just your own. You remind me of my ex Michael with that same bullshit and making decisions that suit yourself. That is so selfish. You could have told me about Pam just like you told me about Shelley. But Denise there was no reason for me to tell you because at the time you and I met, the divorce proceedings were almost finalized until Pam starting saying that James wasn't my son. So we had to go back to court to get that straightened out. You still should have told me about it. Now that I think about it, I remember one time I had Alexis and Greg with me and Greg was telling me that Pam was his stepmother once. Here I am telling Greg, no Pam and your dad just lived together, but they were never married. And Greg kept saying, yes they were. I explained to Greg just because two people live together doesn't mean that they are married. Apparently Greg knew what he was talking about and I didn't. I guess he was confused, or no, I was the confused one and the dumb one. Ugh, you make me sick to my stomach. I'm out of here. Consider the marriage proposal over. It's not going to happen.

A few weeks later I calmed down. Eddie and I talked. I forgave Eddie and decided that we will not break up. One thing I really liked about Eddie is that he knew what I liked. Afterall, we had been together for eight months. We had strong feelings at this point in the relationship and I could not just walk away.

I invited Eddie to my family reunion. We planned to go to Florida afterwards. I wanted Eddie to bring Greg but he decided not to. Eddie wanted a break from his kids.

In late July, me, Eddie, my mother, Alexis and my sister, Tameka drove to my family reunion. When we arrived, it was 104 degrees. As a matter of fact, it was 104 degrees the whole three days we were there. Whew, it was hot as hell!

The first night at the reunion was the welcome night. I introduced Eddie to people in my family. We ate, then went with a few cousins of mine to have a few drinks at a bar. It was fun.

The following day, we had the family cookout. Eddie was playing cards and backgammon with my cousin Jackie.

Later in the evening, we had a formal family dinner in the hotel's ballroom. We had the works. So much good southern food. And very tasty too.

On Sunday morning, most everyone went to the family church and then checked out of the hotel. We stayed another night in our hotel room. The next morning after breakfast, we headed to Florida.

The drive to Disney was long. It was thundering and lightening so much. We saw lightening strike a tree in half and go up in flames. We were tripping.

We arrived in Orlando in the early evening. Once we checked into the hotel, we showered, got something to eat and then headed to the Magic Kingdom to purchase our tickets for the following day.

Alexis woke us up early the next morning. She was so excited about seeing Mickey and Minnie Mouse. After breakfast, we were off to the Magic Kingdom, then to MGM studios. Eddie and Alexis rode the rides. I don't ride. I played all of the games and ate. We watched the Parade on Main Street, Aladdin's Parade and went to the gift shops. We took lots and lots of pictures. It was fun.

When we left Orlando, we drove to Sarasota Springs to check it out. It was beautiful. We decided once we were married, we would buy a summer home there. We ended up getting a hotel room in Sarasota Springs for the night before heading back north.

Chapter 17

I have never been so happy to get home. The drive was long and boring. Eddie dropped me and Alexis home and helped us with the bags. Well, we made it back, Eddie said. Thank God for that. I have to go into town to get Greg from my mother's. Why don't you wait for a little while, I asked. Why? Because I want to take a quick shower and make some dinner for us. Aren't you hungry? Yes, Eddie replied.

After we ate, Eddie left and then I gave Alexis a bath. Within the hour, Alexis was knocked out cold. I unpacked everything. I decided to look at the pictures we took at the family reunion and Disney. They were beautiful.

The phone started ringing. It was Eddie. Hey Hon. Hi baby, what's up? Just checking in. I picked Greg up, unpacked and took a shower. I'm beat as hell. Me too. We talked a little longer then hung up. I got some juice and then went off to bed.

It was hard getting up the next morning for work. I felt like calling in. Once I took a shower, I was fine. I heard the phone ringing. Hi again Hon, Eddie said cheerfully. I want to make sure you got up on time. Eddie was always on time no matter what he did. That's one thing I liked about him. Yeah, I'm up. "I love you," he stated. "I love you too Eddie." Give me a call at work a little later in the day. Eddie said he would, then we hung up.

Before I got settled at work, everyone started asking questions about my vacation. It was great I told them. The whole time we were in the south, it was 104 degrees. Florida was cloudy and very humid.

Hey girlfriend, how goes the battle? I turned around to see who it was. It was Doris. Doris is a loud talking woman from the south, but she was sweet and cool. She had no front teeth in her mouth and two gold teeth on the side. Very spiritual though. Oh, nothing girl. Trying to get situated. Here you go, Doris. I bought a tee shirt and a cap for you from Disney. Thanks Denise. No prob. Let me get myself together Doris and then I will chit chat with you later. Ok, Denise.

I was so busy at work. The work load was heavy due to the upcoming layoffs and retirements. I had stacks of benefit files on my desk for the month of August. I did the benefits administration for the bank and all of the employee benefit changes. By the time 5:00 p.m. rolled around, I was beat. I picked Alexis up from camp, went home to cook, got our clothes together and headed over to Eddie's house. We usually stayed at Eddie's about three times a week.

After Greg and Alexis were in bed for the night, Eddie and I talked. Eddie's lawyer called him earlier and said that the blood test from the paternity tests that were done on him, Greg and Kenny were in. I hope it works out for you, I told him. I know you have strong reservations that Greg isn't your son. Have you thought about what you would do if the tests come back excluding you as the father? If Greg is not mine, he will have to go back to Shelley. Of course I will always love him. Eddie, maybe you would want to consider keeping Greg. Afterall for ten years, you are all he knows as a father and you are his father. That would hurt him and it will also destroy him. I know Denise but it would be the biological father's responsibility to take care of him financially. Do you think Shelley will tell you who he is? No, she probably wouldn't know who the father is. Why not, I asked? For one, Shelley was out there drugging bad and sleeping with different men, just for a quick fix. Get the picture? Yeah. Well I will pray that both Greg and Kenny are your sons. That is terrible you had to go through three paternity test on all three of your sons. Let's pray and get some sleep and hope for the best on tomorrow's paternity outcome. Goodnight.

Chapter 18

Good morning, Eddie said. Good morning beautiful. We both got out of bed and showered together. We made love and showered again together before going to work. I made us some toast with a cup of tea. I'll be in a meeting for most of the morning, I told Eddie. Eddie left for work much earlier than I did.

I got the kids up about 7:00 a.m. each morning. I would make their breakfast and their snack for school. Eddie's oldest son Kenny left early each morning to pick up his girlfriend for school. Kenny rarely ate breakfast.

On this particular morning, I took a good look at Greg. I thought to myself how Greg didn't look anything like Eddie or Kenny. As a matter-of-fact, Kenny and James, Eddie's youngest son, resembled more of each other than Greg and Kenny and they have the same mother, while James has a different mother.

Kenny and James are both light skinned, very tall and slim, just like Eddie. But, Greg is darker, shorter and very stocky. My heart really went out to Greg. He is a very sweet, well mannered kid.

When I would play Kirk Franklin's gospel cd, we would all sing the

The Reason Why I Sing over and over. God, we loved that song! Greg really enjoyed going to church. I asked him one day if he used to go to Sunday school. He said no.

Finally, I was saying goodbye to Greg and telling him to have a good day in school. Within minutes, Alexis and I were out the door. I dropped Alexis off at her school bus stop and I drove to the train station where I parked my car for the day.

When my phone rung, I knew it would be Eddie. Good morning, this is Denise, I answered. Hi Hon. Hi. I just got a call from my lawyer. I was nervous about the results. I pray everything is ok with this paternity test.

What did the lawyer say? Kenny and Greg are my sons. Well A-L-R-I-G-H-T! That's great news Eddie! I know it eases your mind to know that the fear is gone. Yes, it does. Denise, I'm so glad that its over and I can have some peace over this. My concerns have been satisfied finally. I'm happy for you baby. Just imagine if Greg wasn't yours, but Kenny was. That would have torn Greg's world apart. Greg would have had to go back to live with his mother and go to a new school. Not to think of how he would have had to deal with the fact that you weren't his father after ten years of his life. That would have been very devastating. At least we know the truth now. Thank God for DNA testing. Most definitely, Eddie replied.

Eddie I have to go. I'll call you later when you get home from work. Ok honey. I love you. I love you back.

Before I called Eddie back, I called my friend Marcy. She was the only one I confided in and told about the situation. Marcy was glad that everything worked out for Eddie. My other line was clicking. Hold on Marcy. It was Eddie. I clicked back to Marcy and told her I would call her back later.

I could hear the happiness in Eddie's voice. He couldn't stop talking about the results from the paternity tests. I told Eddie that we can finally get on with our lives now that everything has been finalized with the paternity tests.

"Denise, I'll be over your house tonight," Eddie said. "Ok, that would be really nice."

When Eddie arrived, he was all smiles. I gave him a hug. We talked some more about the situation with the boys. I was so happy for Eddie but he started to drive me crazy after a while. Let's just put this chapter behind us and move on, I told him. You are right. Where's Greg? Oh, he's at home with Kenny. I'll be staying the night. Is Alexis asleep? Yes. We went into my room and turned the tv on. Eddie went into the bathroom to take a shower. When he came out of the bathroom, I was already in bed.

Eddie got into the bed. Eddie started massaging my back and then he gave me a foot massage. You are sooooooo beautiful Denise. You are fine, sexy and one hell of a woman. An educated woman too. You believe strongly in God and you have good morals and values about yourself. You have the whole package a man could ask for in a woman. A man would be a fool to have you and to let you go. Well, thank you for the compliments. Why couldn't I have known you earlier in my life? Well it was best if we hadn't known each other then because it wouldn't have worked out. Especially with the past history you had with women. I chuckled. Eddie did not like that comment, but I did not care. I started laughing. Timing is everything boo. "You're right, it is!" You know it.

I knew I had the best man in the world. Eddie and I were so compatible. We are the same zodiac sign, we both had the same color car, we had the same ideas about finances and our goals were very similar.

We took turns cooking and cleaning. We spent a lot of time together as well. Eddie always told me how much he loved me, how beautiful I was and that he definitely wanted me to be his wife. Eddie taught Alexis how to ride her bike, he cooked for her birthday party, he loved her and he treated her like she was his daughter. Eddie treated Alexis like a little princess. He gave her everything.

On the other hand, I cooked for the boys, I watched Greg for Eddie when he had his employee meetings twice a week. I made sure the kids ate a full balanced breakfast before going to school and I accepted his sons as my sons. Technically speaking, we had four kids altogether.

Eddie and I had arguments, but we would be talking and laughing shortly after that. You're a trip Denise, Eddie would say. And so are you.

We decided when we get married we would live off one check and put the other check in the bank. I was happy and I had put on some pounds. My face filled out, my thighs got bigger and I felt complete and whole as a woman. I felt like the luckiest and happiest woman in the world!

I prayed to God. I Thank you God for sending me a good, kind hearted man, who truly loves me for me. Thank you Lord. Bless our soon-to-be-family.

Chapter 19

It was a warm and balmy evening in August. I closed the sliders to my balcony and turned the air conditioner on. I wanted to chill for the evening. I put on R. Kelly's cd and got me a glass of iced cold pepsi.

As I chilled out, I thought about Eddie's situation. I couldn't have been more happier for him.

When the phone ranged, it was Eddie. "What's up," he said? Listening to R. Kelly's c.d. Oh. I could tell Eddie had a sip of something. I hated when he got like that. His attitude was different. "Is everything alright," I asked? "Women." "What about them?" All women are the same and they can't be trusted. Excuse me? Where is all of this coming from Eddie? Talk to me, what's up? I was thinking about all the problems and stupid shit I went through with my exes. Just keep it in the past, I responded. We have a wonderful relationship with each other and we both love each other. Yeah, Denise, they all say that. Have you been sipping on something, Eddie? Yep, why? I knew it. I hate when you have a drink. It changes your whole personality. Like how, he asked? Like for instance, you start loud talking and you start talking off-the-wall shit.

You know Eddie, it seems to me ever since you got the paternity tests results back you have been acting kind of funny with me. I feel like you are pushing me away. And I don't like it. I feel left out.

"Black women are no good," Eddie blurted out. "WHAT," I asked. "What did you say?" "Excuse me." "Man, you are really tripping and really need to lay off the bottle." "Oh Denise, you ain't no saint yourself." "Then you bitches wonder why the brother's turn to the white women." That's bullshit! "But hold up Eddie," wait a minute.

"Did you say bitches?" "Yeah," I did. "I know you are not calling me a bitch?" "Well don't answer to it." "You need to clarify that with me and clarify quickly." And besides, "why are you talking like this?" "What is your fucking problem?" "Please, spare me Denise." "You act like you're all goody-two-shoes." "I just had paternity tests done on my sons." "So and I can understand that, but why are you taking it out on me?" "I did nothing to you." "That's your situation." "Don't blame me." "Blame them."

I explained to Eddie how I'm trying to be there for him and he is pushing me away and shutting me out. He went on and on about not trusting any woman. I felt hurt and I was stunned by the things Eddie was saying. Afterall, this is the man who told me he has never loved anyone like he loves me but yet and still, he is comparing me to his past relationships.

Something was really bothering Eddie. Everytime I tried to talk to him or comfort him, he kept pushing me away. We started to argued a lot, which was something we rarely did. I'm starting to think now about his past relationships. I often wondered why all of the bad blood between his past relationships. Like I said, there is always two sides to a story. Again, I just went along.

I could feel the distance between us. What is happening to us, I asked myself? Out of all the relationships I have had, my relationship with Eddie was very genuine and precious to me. I told Eddie personal things about me that I have never told anyone.

I told Eddie about the time when I was in a relationship with my ex-boyfriend Johnnie, which turned out to be a very jealous relationship. Another time I told Eddie how my daughter, Alexis' father abused me mentally and emotionally by playing mind games with me and trying to get me to have an abortion because he was living a double life that caught up with him, and how he kept the fact from me that he was getting married to someone else, which left a deep scar on me. But, did I take my frustrations out on him? Noooo. That was in the past, I left it in the past and it had nothing to do with my future with Eddie. So what was Eddie's problem? I guess he is looking for someone to blame. Dumb.

How could you act like this towards me Eddie? What have I done to you? Eddie told me he felt alone and wanted to call off the relationship. After we talked some more, we decided that we would not break up. I started getting the feeling that our relationship was going to be like a see-saw – up and down. My stomach knotted up.

I could feel the tension was still there between us. Eddie seemed to have become more arrogant and hard core. He didn't talk to me much. When we did talk, I could tell he had a sip of something. All of a sudden, Eddie did not like talking that much on the phone to me anymore. That was strange. Eddie and I would normally talk for hours on the phone when weren't in the presence of each other. This was becoming mind bottling to me and Eddie was changing. I hope Eddie isn't keeping anything devastating from me because I would not be able to handle another crazy situation. Been there once before and I do not want to go down that road again.

Eddie continued to push me further and further away from him. I would think Eddie would have reacted this way if the paternity tests had proven that the kids were not his or at least Greg was not his. Then I would understand why he would be acting this way. But for things to turn out for the good was beyond me!

Eddie just got the best news in the world. So why was his attitude so fucked up? I decided that I would give myself and Eddie some time alone to think. Something else was going on with him. I could feel it. I had a bad feeling. I know the signs.

When I called Eddie the following day, he was speechless. What's wrong, I would ask? Nothing. Do you want to come over or I come over there so we can talk? No, he said. He sounded so cold when he said no. I think I'm going to get into this ball game a little bit and then go to bed. With hostility in Eddie's voice, he said, Denise I just want to be left alone and do not want to be bothered with you or with anyone at this time!

Alright then, I said. I'll talk to you tomorrow. Before I could say goodnight or goodbye, I heard a click in my ear. What the fuck?

Chapter 20

One evening I decided to go over to my cousin Michelle's house to visit. When I got there, a few friends that we had grown up with were there. We talked about old times, our careers and men.

Michelle had finger food for us to nibble on. We laughed and joked for over two hours. It was getting late. I decided I am going to head out.

When I left, I dropped my friend Andrea off at home. It was on my way going home. After I dropped Andrea off, I drove down Druids Hills. I thought about my friend Charles. Charles was cool and I had not seen him in a while, so I decided to drop by for a few minutes to say hello.

I pulled up into his driveway and blew my horn. Charles looked out the window. "It's Denise, what's up?" "You busy?" "Naw girl," he said. "Then, come downstairs for a minute." "I'll be right there," Charles said.

Within minutes, Charles was downstairs. We said hello. "I haven't seen you in so long Denise." "Yeah I know." "What's up my nigger," I said jokingly. "What's up woman," he replied. "Nothing but the sky," I laughed. "Denise you are still a trip." "And you still have that great sense of humor." "I try, I try." We both burst out with laughter. "Hey, I was just chilling on it for a bit." "Chilling on what, may I ask?" "You know me Denise, when I am not on duty, I get zooted up!" "You hear me, girl!" "Zooted up!" This brother was off the chain. I could tell Charles had the munchies from being high off of something, most likely it was some weed. "Why don't you come up Denise," Charles asked? "I don't want my chicken to burn." "Alright, let me park my car."

Charles had his small apartment laid out for a guy. "I asked him how is his family doing, if he is dating and how is his job?" "Everything's good homie." "You're too funny Charles," I said. "So Denise, what's up with you?" "How are you and Eddie doing these days," Charles asked? "Oh we are ok I guess." "What do you mean, you guess?" We are having a few problems but nothing that would break us up. Well, that's good. But you know what Charles, Eddie is so damn demanding and very dominant. That's the one thing I don't like about him. He wants to be in control of everything. It drives me crazy at times. Don't get me wrong. Eddie is a good person and he is very good to me, but it's when he gets this kind of attitude is when I really cannot deal with him. Sometimes I want to get out of the relationship, you know. "Yeah, I see your point Denise," Charles said. "I know you." "You will listen to a person, bend over backwards for a person and when you are down for a person, you will definitely give the shirt off of your back." "But I do understand there is only so much you can and will take." "You're right Charles." "I knew you would understand me," I replied. After talking to Charles for an hour and watching him getting zooted off of his weed and getting his drink on, it was time for me to go.

I told Charles I was about to bounce. "Why are you leaving?" "Because Eddie is probably trying to call me?" "Before I leave, can I have some water?" "Sure no problem," Charles said. Charles gave me a bottled water.

After I dranked the water, I went towards the door to open it. Charles blocked the door. "What the hell are you doing," I asked? "Why are you leaving so soon?" "Soon Charles, please." "I have been here over an hour." "Besides, I need to get home because it's late and Eddie is probably trying to reach me." "Damn girl, you are so fine," Charles said. "Thank you, but I have to go." "Oh, come on Denise don't go." "Sorry Charles, but I have to."

Charles grabbed my arm and was trying to pull me towards him. He was high as a kite. "Get the fuck off of me and move out of my way," I yelled! "You sure are a tough cookie Denise." "Boy, please!" "Now move." "I have to get out of here." "I have been gone for a long time and I know Eddie is wondering where the hell I could be." I know Eddie is fuming right about now. How am I going to explain to Eddie where I have been all of this time after I left Michelle's? Charles pulled his pants down and showed me his nasty looking shit. Ugh! I slapped the fuck out of Charles, broke away from him and left out of the front door. I called Charles a stupid ass. He just laughed. Girl, you know I'm just messing around with you. I asked myself, "how am I going to explain the long period of time to Eddie?" Fuck it. I'm going to tell Eddie the truth. There is no need for me to lie to him about my whereabouts. I'm a grown ass woman.

Eddie and I have always said that we would be honest with each other about any and everything. I thought to myself, "everything is going so wrong." Eddie is acting funny and pushing me way out in left field. If Eddie hadn't been acting fucked up lately and pushing me the fuck away, I wouldn't have been put in this predicament in the first place. But, I wasn't going to use that as an excuse. Shit, I'm grown.

Why was this happening to me? "Why I asked myself?" All hell is going to break loose sooner or later. I can feel it.

When I got home, I took a long bath. I meditated. That's it. It's final. I am going to tell Eddie. The only thing is that Eddie only likes to see things his way and only hears what he wants to hear. He blows things way out of proportion. That's the problem I have with him. Either Eddie will believe me or he won't. I prayed to God that I was making the right decision by telling Eddie. I felt it in my heart that I was.

Chapter 21

It was a nice day on Saturday. I was at Eddie's house with Alexis. The boys were out for the day. Alexis was in the basement playing with her toys and then she asked if she could take her bike out.

While Alexis was riding her bike, Eddie and I were in the kitchen talking. Eddie wanted to make love to me. I told him I didn't feel like doing that shit. I had no desire whatsoever. "I need to talk to you Eddie." "Ok, because you sure as hell have been acting funny and withdrawn the past few days." "So what's up, Denise?" I told Eddie the whole story. We went outside in the backyard and sat at the picnic table. Eddie told me he had a feeling something wasn't right when he hadn't heard from me. It's just that I felt so alone, so I decided to go to Michelle's for a while. After I left, I dropped Andrea off at home and then I decided to stop by to say hello to my friend Charles. Eddie was pissed with me. You mean to tell me you went over another nigger's house? Yeah, but it's no big deal. Nothing happened. Dang, I said. That's not the fucking point, Denise. You are wrong for that. Eddie, I am not going to go back and forth with you on this. Out of respect for one another and the relationship, I just wanted to tell you this. Again, it's no big deal. Jesus.

Later that evening, we went to Unos to eat. I couldn't eat neither could Eddie. I knew this hurt Eddie and messed him up in the head. I didn't feel bad because I felt I hadn't done anything wrong or out of character. Shit, I went to visit a friend. After we discussed the situation some more, Eddie told me he still wants us to get married. "Let me ask you a question Eddie?" "Why would you want to still marry me after what I just told you?" He answered, "because I love you and I can forgive you for this." "This isn't all your damn fault Denise." "Although you had no fucking business going over to another nigger's house because of some bullshit you got in your head about what's going on with me." I just looked at Eddie and rolled my eyes.

"Eddie, you know what?" "I may have been wrong for going over Charles' house, but again that is how I reacted because of the way you were treating me." "But two wrongs don't make a right, you know." "I'm sorry," I said. "I should have known better." "I hope you can really forgive me so that we can move forward." "Yes, I can forgive you Denise." "Thank you," I said.

By 10:00 p.m., Eddie and I were back at my house. Eddie told me to get some rest and that he will be home if I needed him. "Thank you for listening to me and believing in me Eddie." "I love you." "I love you too, Denise."

"Make sure you get your rest Denise," Eddie said. I smiled and reassured Eddie that I would.

Chapter 22

$\mathcal{M}$y relationship with Eddie started going downhill and was taking a turn for the worse. He had more excuses than anyone I have ever known, besides Michael.

A few days before Christmas, Eddie's youngest son James asked him what was under the Christmas tree for them and Eddie responded by saying, "you all always want to know what I got you for guys." "What about me?" "My father never cared to asked me anything." "In fact, he wasn't even in my life." Eddie had tears in his eyes. The next thing I knew he was in the bathroom wiping his face. When he came out of the bathroom, he went outside and stood on the front steps. I followed him. "What's wrong Eddie?" He looked at me with teary eyes. "Denise, I'm not the person you think I am." "What are you talking about?" "Trust me, I'm not." I had a frown on my face and started thinking to myself, what does that mean? Like, what's the problem? Eddie did not say another word, so I left it alone.

The night before Christmas, I called Eddie to come over to put Alexis' dollhouse together.

After the dollhouse was assembled, Eddie said he had to go because the two little ones, Greg and James were still awake and he did not want them snooping around the Christmas tree. I told Eddie to call me when he gets home so I will know that he made it home safely.

I noticed an half hour later Eddie had not called. He only lived two miles down the street from me. What was taking him so long? I decided to call. Greg answered the phone. "Hey Greg, where is your dad?" "He's not here Denise." "Alright, he should be there in a few minutes." "Don't open the door for anyone." "Ok, I won't." Then I hung up.

I figured Eddie probably stopped at the neighborhood pub for a drink. But he would not do that with Greg and James there in the house alone and for that length of time. Or would he? At 12:30 a.m., I called again. Greg answered. Did your father get in? No, he said. "Where is Kenny," I asked? "Kenny is not here and James is sleeping." "Did Eddie ever come back since I called the first time?" "No." "Did he call you guys?" "No, he didn't." Thanks Greg. I will see you all in the morning. Goodnight.

My mind was racing and wondering now. Where the hell is Eddie? He made such a big deal to get home and didn't even go home. I kept calling and calling. Finally, I woke up at 4:00 a.m. I dialed Eddie's number. His sleepy voice answered. H-e-l-l-o. "Eddie, it's me," I yelled! "Merry Christmas honey," he said. I ignored that. "Where the hell were you?" "I was here." Not, I said. "You never came home when you left my house." "Denise, I came home, took a shower and then passed out." Naw, that's not what you did. It would have seem to me that Greg would have known you were there sleeping. You are fucking lying. Where were you, I asked again? I went to visit some friends. Friends, huh? Oh, you would rather spend Christmas Eve with friends rather than your lady? Denise, you're making such a big deal out of nothing. No, I'm not, I yelled. I'll talk to you in the morning Eddie. I just hung up the phone.

The phone ranged. Hello. Good morning, Merry Christmas, I answered. Merry Christmas honey. Is Alexis up? Yes, she is. I still felt hostile towards Eddie. I told Eddie that we will be over later to bring the gifts. I have to wait for my mother, Tameka and Linda to get here. Did you want to come to my family's Christmas dinner at 4:00 p.m. today? I don't know Eddie. Alright. See you in a bit. Click.

Once we got to Eddie's house, we exchanged our gifts. I bought all the boys Rocawear shirts and footballs. I got Eddie an expensive watch and a nice Gucci leather wallet. In return, Eddie gave Alexis a pair of gold earrings and gave me a beautiful 14k gold bracelet. It was worth some dough. Eddie even bought my sister Tameka a gold bracelet. How sweet of him. But still, something was missing and was definitely wrong.

Later that evening, all of us, including my friend Linda went to Eddie's family's Christmas dinner. It was fun. There was plenty of food. I gave Eddie's mother a Bath & Body Works basket with different kinds of perfumed soaps and gels.

On our way home, I felt distant from Eddie. Linda asked me I was going to stay at Eddie's tonight. I'm not sure. I felt something in my gut that just wasn't right. I wanted to stay but Eddie gave me the impression that he didn't want me to.

We dropped Linda off and said our goodbyes.

After we dropped Linda off, Eddie and I didn't say one word to each other. Finally, I asked Eddie what seems to be the problem. "Nothing," he answered. When Alexis and I got dropped off, we all said goodnight. I just slammed the car door shut and went upstairs. I did not look back.

Chapter 23

It was the afternoon of New Year's Eve. My best friend Linda got sick and I went with her to the clinic. Linda is a very paranoid person. She always thinks the worst. The bottom line is that everything check out to be fine. Linda was cool though.

Denise, why don't you call Eddie to see what's up for tonight? I don't know about that Linda. Eddie's been acting very stupid and fucked up lately. He told me he was thinking that maybe we should break up. I really don't understand him. You know men, Linda said jokingly. Yeah, but Eddie keeps going back and forth with this. All he has to do is be honest with me and tell me what the hell is really going on or what is really bothering him. It's simple as that.

Let me call him. Eddie picked up his phone. What's up Eddie? Nothing. I want to know if you wanted to go out tonight to celebrate the New Year coming in. Naw, I think I'm going to chill at home. Why? Because Denise, I think we should go our separate ways. What? You want to say that again? Because I am not understanding that right now, Eddie. I really don't feel like getting into this right now Denise. Call me later and maybe I'll change my mind about going out. Bye. Click. Damn. Eddie is getting stranger and stranger by the day.

Linda and I headed to the mall after we left the hospital. I needed to find a black velour dress just in case we decided to go out. When we left the mall, we headed to Linda's house so she could pick up her clothes. She was staying at my house that night.

Later that evening I talked to Eddie. We had this big argument. It's over Denise, Eddie shouted! It is O-V-E-R. I don't want to talk about it or discuss this anymore. I'm done. And, I am not answering any lame questions either! You got that? Ok fine, if this is what you want, you got it. Happy New Year Eddie. I hope you get all you're looking for. Take care. Eddie just hung up in my face! Cold.

Denise, Eddie is crazy. What is wrong with him, Linda asked? He keeps going back and forth with this. Damn be a man and say what the fuck is up. I agree Linda. You know what, I don't care Linda. If Eddie really wants it to be over, then fine. I'm not kissing nobody's ass. I wonder why he's acting like that? Girl, I don't know. He claims to love me so much. We planned for our wedding to be in September but now it's off. Eddie claims he loves me so much, but yet and still he broke it off. And for what reason or reasons. He still hasn't told you anything. Eddie seem like he's confused. Linda, he's not confused. Something else is going on here. You know what, I think Eddie's pattern is hooking up with women, treating them like a queen, getting them hook and then he leaves them out of the blue. He just drops them like a hot potatoe! And, he leaves them wounded and hurting.

So much for us going out to celebrate New Year's Eve. I decided to lay down until 11:50 p.m. Let me know when it's ten minutes till twelve Linda. I'll get up and say Happy New Year to you. Alright, I'm going to watch some tv.

I must have been so tired because when I was awaken by my doorbell,

I looked at the clock and it read 2:00 a.m. I wonder who this could be ringing my doorbell this time of morning. I got up. Linda, did you hear my doorbell ring? Yeah. I wonder who it is? Let's find out. I press the intercom and spoke into it. Hello. It's Eddie. Oh shit Linda! It's Eddie! I wonder what he wants at this time of the morning? I buzzed him in.

I opened the door. Eddie looked in my eyes and said, "Denise, I couldn't bring in the new year without you." It felt weird. While I was driving around, I thought to myself why should I see whatelse is out there, when I already know what I have with you. "Hmmm," I said. For some reason I really didn't believe Eddie. "Again Denise, I don't know what I would be getting out there but I know what I already have with you." Denise, that's when I realized that I wanted us to stay together. Are you sure, Eddie? "Yes baby, I'm sure." Because for one, I can't keep going back and forth with you. If there is something bothering you, we need to talk about it and get to the bottom of whatever it is you are going through. I'm good. I just had a lot on my mind from the paternity tests and all. Eddie poured a drink for him and Linda. We all talked for an hour, then we got ready for bed.

When Eddie and I went into my room, we talked. Are you and Alexis going to move in with me and the boys? Huh? I thought we were going to wait until we get married to move it? I know Denise but I think it would be good for us to live together and now is the time. Ok, yes if that is what you truly want us to do. Of course it is, Denise. Ok then, yes we will move in with you and the boys. It doesn't make any sense for you to be paying nine hundered dollars a month for rent and my mortgage being twelve hundred dollars a month, Eddie added. Why pay all this money, when we can save. Yeah, that's true. Plus, we need money for the wedding in September. I agree with you Eddie. Tomorrow I will call the office and let them know that I am giving my thirty day notice and that I will be moving out the end of the month. Ok cool. Sounds good to me.

You know Eddie, we should shop at BJ's once a month. It's easier than going into the grocery store every week. True that, he agreed.

We got into bed and made love. But for some reason, it wasn't the same for me anymore. Something wasn't quite right. I could sense it and I could feel it. But leave it up to Eddie, everything is all good. The next morning I fixed us a big breakfast. Eddie told me that he will meet me at my mom's house.

Eddie met me and Linda at my mother's for dinner. After we left my mom's, we all went over to his aunt's house. Eddie's aunt complimented me on how pretty I was and how nice I looked. She made a drink for Eddie and for Linda. I really did not drink, so I passed. After an hour or so of mingling with the family members, we left.

We dropped Linda off and then headed home.

Chapter 24

*W*hat, I shouted! I got a call from my mother saying that my cousin Jerome was found dead in his apartment. Mom, what happened? Apparently the tenants thought Jerome was at the drug/ alcohol treatment center for three weeks since they haven't seen or heard from him. They said usually when he is not around, that is where he is.

The landlord, Mrs. Brothers went to Jerome's apartment to ask why he had not paid his rent. When Mrs. Brothers got upstairs, she noticed his door was cracked open a little. She pushed the door open and noticed Jerome's whole face was swollen and his skin color was bluish-purple, then the strong odor hit her. Mrs. Brother's screamed and ran downstairs and knocked on another neighbor's door. Then they called the police.

When the paramedics arrived, they called the medical examiner. The medical examiner pronounced Jerome dead. It was declared that Jerome was dead for three weeks. His pants were down to his knees. Like, why? What was that about? Did he try going to the restroom or something?

I wonder if Jerome had a heart attack, I asked? I don't know Denise. Well you know Jerome drinks heavy and definitely an alcoholic. I don't know if he was trying to get to the bathroom and a heart attack came on him and he just fell on the bed. That is a damn a shame. Shit, it is!

When we spoke with the people at the drug/alcohol treament center, they told us that Jerome was a heavy drug and alcohol user. I told them that we knew about the alcohol but not the drugs.

An autopsy was performed on Jerome. The results came back stating that Jerome definitely died from alcohol poisoning. That wasn't a shocker to me. My mother said that she was going to notify the family and we would start preparing for the funeral arrangements. Damn, dead for three weeks without anyone knowing.

I called Eddie and told him what I just found out. Really? That's messed up. I told you Jerome drinks a lot. This time Jerome dranked himself to death.

The funeral was scheduled for a week later. Jerome's brother Carl and his wife Marshell came up. All the first cousins were there. My grandmother didn't come. She can't travel long distance anymore. And my aunt Mabel who is Jerome's mother was in the hospital at the time so she could not make it. It was a snowy day and very cold. The funeral was very small. Just the family members. Eddie came to support me. After everything was over, Eddie went back to work and we went back to my mom's house to eat. I promised Eddie that I would bring him and Greg a plate of food. He kissed me before we left for the burial site.

Chapter 25

A week later after Jerome's funeral, Eddie called me up with some bad, crazy news. When I answered the phone and heard his voice, I knew something was wrong. Usually when Eddie called, he is very cheerful. This time, it was different.

Hi Denise, he said. Hi. I'm sorry, but I don't want the relationship anymore. What, why? What happened? Nothing, I just don't want the relationship. I feel pressured. Pressured, I shouted! Why would you feel pressured? I just do. But why? You're not making sense Eddie. Ok, Eddie talk to me. This is me you are talking to. Tell me what's up. Don't do this to me. Things have been going so well for us. Are you getting cold feet about getting married? Just let me know. Don't do this to me Eddie, don't. We have always been able to communicate openly with one another. Don't shut me out like this. Please, tell me what's up. Eddie went silent.

I need to get myself together. I need to get into myself more and into my inner feelings. Okay, so you need to break it off for that reason, Eddie? Yes, I do. Oh no, that's some bullshit right there. I think something else is going on with you. Denise, I'm trying to get more into my boys and into God. Great, that's a good thing. Well, we can get into God together, I told him.

"No," Eddie shouted! "I want to do it alone." "I have to do this alone." "I don't want any woman around me when I do this." "So Denise, thanks but no thanks." Eddie, whoa! "What the hell is going on here?" "Talk to me, please!" "Denise, please, by all means, just try to accept it and move on with your life." I frowned. I was totally lost and totally confused by Eddie. "You and I are no longer happening." "Well that is fine, but can you give me a better explanation than what you are giving me?" "Listen, I have to go right now." "Goodbye Denise," Eddie said. The next thing I heard was another click in my ear. My heart was racing, my head was spinning and my life was about to crumble.

I was stunned by Eddie's behavior. This wasn't Eddie at all. Something didn't seem right. My curiosity was kicking me in the ass. I called Eddie back.

Eddie, I said sadly. I need to talk to you! Tell me the real reason why you want to break up with me. I have already told you Denise. But that's bullshit and you know it. So you going to use God for your escape?

Look, I just got in from work and I have things to do. I understand that, but please tell me what's going on with you.

Just go on with your life. But just last week you asked me and Alexis to move in with you guys. Now you're saying you don't want the relationship and to just move on with my life. Yes, that's exactly what I am saying. Click.

I called Eddie back. Listen Eddie please. Hear me out! If you would just tell me the real truth, I would understand better. I did Denise, you just won't accept it. I told you I want to get more into God, my boys and myself. Your boys? You have always been into your boys. My God, you have sole custody of your boys. "Ok, so when did you decide on all of this?" It's been on my mind for a while. Oh really, I stated. Yes, really.

Can I ask you something Eddie? "What," he shouted! Why are you yelling and getting so defensive Eddie? "What is it Denise?", he asked? Is it another woman? No and I can honestly say no. Eddie, you at least owe me the real truth. I told you three or four times already. Well, I don't buy that story. Well then Denise, that's up to you. Why are you so cold hearted all of a sudden towards me? I'm not, Eddie said. Yes, you are.

What's up then? I am about to move out of my apartment, we are in the process of making plans for our future, thinking of buying a house together and you're going to throw it all away just like that? Yes, I am. Goodbye Denise and he hung up.

Chapter 26

I was so hurt and so confused. I fell on the bed and started crying. My heart ached. I started back tracking about some things. Particularly with this woman name Monica.

I remember around Christmas time Eddie received a card from her. It was a card with words saying "Thinking of you and only you at Christmas time." I questioned Eddie about this then, but he told me I was making such a big deal out of nothing. I didn't feel this way, but I let it go. That was a sign right there in my face. I just ignored it.

Sometimes when the phone would ring at Eddie's and whenever I answered, the person on the other end would hang up. I suspect it was that woman Monica.

One day when I went by Eddie's house to talk to him. While he was in the shower, I found his phone book and looked up Monica's phone number. I found it and wrote down the number on a piece of paper. When Eddie got out of the shower, we talked some more, but I didn't get anywhere with him.

Later that evening, I called Eddie. His line was busy. I hung up and dialed Monica's number. I could tell she was on the other line. When she answered, I simply said, "find your own man and leave mine alone," then I hung up. That's to let her know that I know what's up.

Within an half hour, Eddie called me. I knew I was on the right track then. Eddie asked me if I called his "so called" friend, Monica. Yes, I did. Is there some kind of problem? Why did you do that? Because I'm trying to find some answers, which you won't give me. And this is the way you do it? Yes, it is. And besides, I always follow my instincts. You know that better than anyone. But why are you calling to bother Monica? We're just friends and you have no right calling up my friends. Sure you're right, I said with a smirk. You better stop it Denise. Yeah right.

At that very moment, Eddie got really pissed with me. He said, "you didn't mess anything up." "Well Eddie, I didn't think there was anything to mess up or is there?" Get your lies straight when you're talking to me buddy. You just made yourself look like a damn fool Denise. I don't think so baby. Don't call me baby Denise. I'm not your baby. Ha, what a joke! Just a few weeks ago you were. Well that was then, this is now. Get a life. Oh really, get a life! I have a life.

"So this is the so called friend, Monica you told me about before when I questioned you about the Christmas card?" "Yeah and she's just a friend." "That's nice," I said. Some friend. "I don't believe one word you are telling me." "That's your fucking problem," Denise. Isn't this the woman you said was involved with a married man and he told her he has no plans on leaving his wife or daughter for her? Yes, your fucking point being? I ignored what Eddie just said and kept talking. And isn't this the same woman you claim you needed to talk to other than me to get a different view of opinion about what's happening in our relationship? Yep, Eddie said being funny. And if I'm not mistaken, isn't this the woman who told you that you should leave me since we don't have any kids together? So what? What are you saying Denise?

Did you say, so what Eddie? Are you serious and are you kidding me? What I am saying to you Eddie is that you are a fucking liar and you have been dealing with this Monica person all along. Oh yeah, I finally got the picture. No you don't Denise. Oh yeah Eddie, I do. Be a man and admit it. You are busted! Girl, please. Go on with that.

The next week, I was so hurt because I had finally put my finger on the right button. I was devastated. So one night about 11:00, I decided to get up and drive down Eddie's street. Sure enough, parked right in Eddie's driveway behind his car, was Monica's little beat up box of a car.

Don't panick I said to myself. Don't jump to any conclusions. I drove back home sobbing in tears. Why would he do this, I asked myself? What's the matter with him? Is he tripping?

I decided to drive down Eddie's street two more times; once at 2:00 a.m. and once at 6:00 a.m. Monica's car was still parked there in that very same parking spot. This not only indicated to me that she was just visiting, but she had spent the night with Eddie. How could he have another woman in his bed after I was just there two weeks ago? Is this what I meant to him after all? "Why would Monica hop into Eddie's bed so quickly?" She knew we were together, without a doubt. She did not care. She told me so. Monica had been there with Eddie before. This is not the first time. Bottom line.

I was fuming. I dialed Eddie's phone number. Each time I called him, he would hang up in my face. Eventually he turned the ringer off. I decided to call his son, Kenny on his phone line. Hi Kenny, it's Denise. Will you ask your father to turn his ringer back on and to pick up the phone? Denise, I think he's asleep. His room door is closed. You know how he gets if he's disturbed. That's true Kenny. Ok, no problem. Thank you.

119

Let him know I called and that I know his "so called" friend, Monica is there with him. That's wrong, I said.

Kenny said to me, "I understand." "I can't tell my father what to do, but that's not right." You were just here with us. You were good to me and Greg. It would have been so nice if you and Alexis were going to move in with us. I know Kenny. Don't you worry about that. Maybe she will get up and leave early in the morning before you and Greg get up. I don't think so Denise. I paused, then said to Kenny, "whatever you do in life, do not ever be with a woman who is so easy to get into bed, because if she is that easy and like that with you, you better believe she was like that with her last, the one before him and will be like that with the next one after you." Take care Kenny.

When I hung up from Kenny, I realized that this had to be going on for some time. Why would a woman hop into another man's bed so quickly, especially when she knows he was just in a committed relationship with someone else and then broke it off so abruptly at that? Where are her standards and self respect as a woman? Or did she not have any or simply didn't give a damn? Maybe it's both.

No decent man wants a woman of this nature. He may mess around with her and take her to bed for good times, but when it comes to meeting his family or being his wife, she will not be the one! She's not a keeper in the long run. Boy was I fooled.

Chapter 27

I was at home one day watching tv and my phone rings. "Hello," I answered. "May I speak with Denise?" "This is Denise," who's speaking please?

"You know who this is," you B-I-T-C-H. I thought to myself, "this must be Monica." "How did she get my number," I wondered? "Oh, I know all too well how she got my number." She went through Eddie's phone book. "Well what do you want," I asked?

"Listen Denise you stupid ass bitch," "you got one more fucking time." "Just one more fucking time!" "You better be glad I'm at work because otherwise I would come over there and drop your dumb ass." And you're just jealous because you're not getting it anymore. "Honey, I'm getting it all night long." Then Monica starts singing Lionel Ritchie's song "All Night Long." Crazy whore. What a ding bat. A project ass hoe.

Monica, "let me tell you something you bald headed whore." "You just sold yourself short by calling me and telling me what type of a woman you really are." "It's a damn shame to know that all it takes to make you happy is for a man to fuck you and you are satisfied." There are no requirements for you. You just lay down for them. You are a low down dirty woman. "A slut." "A whore." "Where are your values and self respect?" "Oops, I forgot you don't have any." "My bad." You are so beneath me, Monica. You don't stand in my line of class. If you were to stand next to me, you would melt. Don't you have some kind of respect for yourself? Oops, I forgot again. Ugh, silly me. "Why, did I ask the same stupid ass question again?" Of course you don't have any respect for yourself. After all, "weren't you with a married man and tried to screw his marriage up but that man came to his senses and realized that all you are is just a nasty ass, sleezy ass street woman and who is definitely not worth it?" "You are like a revolving door when it comes to men." "Knock knock, open wide as they say." You need to go get yourself checked out.

Thank God that man woke up and left your nasty ass alone and made amends with his wife. Maybe if you change your conniving and corruptive ways and find a man who is available and leave other women men alone, you would have better luck with men and relationships. You are a homewrecker. You will get what's coming to you in the end. "At this point," Monica cut me off. "Listen Denise," fuck Eddie. I am already two steps ahead of Eddie. If it works, it works. If it doesn't, it doesn't. There are more fish in the sea. "See that is the difference between you and me," Denise. My eyes are wide open where Eddie is concern. I have been around the block a couple of times and I know what type of man Eddie is and how to deal with him. You Denise on the other hand, is blind and this is why you did not see what was coming to your simple ass. You want me to give you a crash course? I clicked on her ass at this point. This hoe is crazy. When Eddie got home from work, I called him to tell him about the phone call I received from Monica. As soon as he heard my voice, he hung up. I called again, but he hung up again. Eddie did not want to hear anything I was saying. He did not even give me a chance. I just wanted to tell him what type of woman he is dealing with.

Oh well, if that's what Eddie wants that's what he will get. She will end up screwing him in the end. I can guarantee you that.

I was hurting bad. It felt like I had been stabbed in the back twice. Everything had fallen apart for me. My dreams, plans and my life. Things couldn't have gotten any better. I had just been laid off from my job at the bank, I was devastated and I was completely lost. Eddie broke off the relationship and the wedding and now the woman he told me about as his friend, he's seeing her and sexing her. To top things off, Eddie and I lived in the same town, only two miles away. That's deep. "How am I going to get past this?" My whole life is crushed.

Everyone tried to comfort me and told me things would get better. Easier said than done, I thought to myself. I can't begin to move on. "What am I going to do?"

I remembered when this woman Jeanette told me that this would be the perfect time for me to start an intimate relationship with God. I agreed and decided that in time I would. But right now, my priority was my situation with Eddie. I wasn't trying to hear anything else at this time. I needed to handle this. This is where I went wrong – I put my situation before God. I kept stumbling and stumbling, but never falling. God is with me and carrying me. I just didn't seem to get this at all.

Chapter 28

*F*inally spoke to Eddie. Boy, was he hot with me when I told him what I knew, about his lies and about this woman. He called me all kinds of nasty names. He broke me down mentally. He was like night and day. A few months back, he was so in love with me and wanted to me marry and this week, he act like he hated me and couldn't stand me.

All you had to do was be honest with me. I was crying like a baby. Eddie kept hanging up on me.

"Look for the last time Denise," "do not call me," "don't come near my house" and "stay away from my family." I don't love you anymore, in fact, I don't even like you. You're a pain in the ass. I thought Pam was a pain, but you're worst than she is. Now for the last time, IT'S OVER, NOW MOVE ON AND GET A LIFE! Oh yeah and find yourself another job. That's your problem, you have too much time on your hands. Click. I was in shock. I just held the phone to my ear with my mouth wide opened. I could not believe the things Eddie was saying. Just like that, out of the blue.

I called right back. Denise, you have a serious problem. You need some help. You're a sick bitch. I hate you he said. And I don't ever in my entire life want to be with you. Move on and forget about me!

Every time I tried to voice my opinion, Eddie would either cut me off or hang up. He would not listen to me at all. "Was this the Eddie who had treated my with respect and like a queen, who was in love with me and who share everything with me?" "What happened?" I just couldn't believe this was the same Eddie that I loved.

I decided to go over to Eddie's house. I figured once he saw me rather than hear my voice on the phone, he would talk to me. Wrong.

I rung the doorbell. Eddie looked out of the side of his window. When he saw that it was me, he started yelling like a mad, crazy dog. Get away from my damn door Denise, he said! I need to talk to you. There's nothing else to say, now go. Yes there is, I yelled. You owe my an explanation. I don't owe you shit! Don't start that crying act Denise because it won't work with me. Save the bullshit! And if you don't get away from my door, I'm calling the police. Go ahead, I don't care. I was really sobbing.

Within moments I heard sirens and then two police cruisers pulled into Eddie's driveway. Hi, the officers said to me. Eddie opened the door. What's the problem here, sir? Eddie explained his side of the story and I explained mine. I want her off of my property. She's trespassing and invading my privacy. What, I said. Oh my God, he's lying.

The officers told me I had to leave Eddie's property. One of the officer's pulled me aside and said Eddie is being a coward and to let things cool down, then see what happens. I agreed and left.

When I got home, I called Eddie to tell him what a jerk he was. He wouldn't listen. When I called back, he let his answering machine pick up.

As time went on, things got crazier than they already were. Eddie called the police on me again. This time, the officer said if they are called again to Eddie's residence regarding me, they would have to arrest me. The next thing I knew, I received a summons in the mail to go to court. Eddie had taken out a restraining order against me.

That did it for me. I thought, he's the one who's crazy and has a serious problem. Not me. This is his pattern with women – love them, romance and leave them at the drop of a dime! Now I completely understand about what happened between his first and second wives. It was him. Not them. I definitely get it now. Again, there are always two sides to a story and I only heard Eddie's side. And I know he is telling this Monica chick all kinds of made up horrible things about me. And she too, is dumb and will believe every word he is saying to her until her day comes. Then, she too will be his next victim.

I didn't show up for court. A couple of days later, I got a copy of the restraining order in the mail. It simply stated that I am not to go within 100 feet of Eddie, his house, or his job for one year. I called Eddie and told him what he did was unnecessary and that he is dead wrong. Of course, he cussed me out again and called me all kinds of names. He's so disrespecful. In the background, I could hear Eddie and his dumb chick laughing at me. They both blurted out with laughter, "see ya wouldn't wanna be ya." "I got the man now," Monica said. "Not you." "Bye bitch." Click. I thought I was having a bad dream but this was R-E-A-L.

A week later, Eddie and Monica were married. I was crushed. How could he marry someone else so quickly after he broke it off with me? The answer came to me quickly. She was already there on the side all along. Monica knew about me, I just didn't know about her until it all unraveled. Monica was Eddie's back up plan. I was crushed. I let it go. Afterall, Eddie said he didn't like me, couldn't stand me and he hated me. Hate is a strong word. I held onto those words and that's what made me go on and made me stronger. So much for Prince Charming.

Chapter 29

started getting back into church. One Sunday the pastor's message was so powerful, when it came time for the invitation for membership, I got up and joined! I was so moved by the holy spirit that day.

I felt so relieved. It felt like all of my hurt, my pain and my problems were lifted from me. The ushers escorted me and a few other people who had gotten up to join the church out of the main santuary into a small office.

We all filled out a form that asked questions - name, address, have you ever been baptized, etc. I had never been baptized.

Once all the forms were completed, we were told that the New Members Class will start on Monday. I was there. I learned so much. I was really into it. It seemed that the hurt and the pain was getting easier and easier, hour by hour, day by day.

On March 24th, I was baptized. I was nervous but one of the deaconnesses told me not to be because this is the best water I could get into because it was holy water.

Amazingly, I was amazed that I was the first one to be called for baptism. Why me? Was it that obvious I needed this. Lol!

I remembered as I was stepping into the water, it was very cold and everyone was singing "Take Me to the Water." The pastor and a few deacons of the church were also in the water. When I was fully in the pool, the lights were dimmed. My family and the other candidates families were around the pool, along with other witnesses. Reverend Dubois asked me if I was ok. I told him that I was but I was nervous as well. The Reverend gave me some comforting words then asked me if I wanted to let someone else go before me. No, I said. I'm not turning back now. I have come too far to turn around.

At that moment, Reverend Dubois said a prayer, told me to cross my arms across my chest and hold my breath. I did. The next thing I knew I was dipped under water and brought up immediately. I stepped out of the pool and a white sheet was placed around me. Juliette, who was my sheppard, hugged me saying, "you did it, you did it." I was in tears. All I remembered was when I came up from being dipped under water, I opened my eyes and the ceiling of the church appeared to me like heaven was being opened. It was the most amazing experience I ever had experienced. I have always heard when being baptized, everyone will experience something different. It must be true.

After being baptized, I continued to attend services every Sunday and started paying my tides. I felt good. I had smiled, which was something I couldn't do too often after the breakup. I was starting to find myself.

The bottom line with Eddie is that he meets women to his liking, he wines them and dines them, loves them and then leaves them, only to be scarred. Then he is on to the next victim. This is Eddie's game. I will pray for the next victim, who happens to be Monica. She doesn't know what she's about to get herself into. But then again, Monica did say she is already two steps ahead of Eddie. She is playing her cards right. Maybe Eddie doesn't know what he's getting himself into. I think Eddie my have met his match this time around.

In my own thoughts and for my own piece of mind, I forgave Eddie. Not for him, but for me. I didn't hate him. In fact, I still loved him just not in love with him. I was going to let the good Lord handle that. I took it completely out of my hands. I felt free for the first time in a very long time. I'm actually finding myself.

Chapter 30

It's been a whole year since I was saved and baptized. I received a call from my friend Carmen. Denise, guess who got baptized at my church today? Who I asked? Eddie. I paused. Are you sure Carmen? Yes, I know what Eddie looks like. I know you do, girl. Well that's good for him, I said. Afterall, he said he wanted to get into God. I hope he's going to do the right thing. Maybe he will Carmen said.

One day I was at home trying to decide where to go from here. When I analyzed my situation, I had been laid off from the bank and had nothing to lose. It was time for me to start planning to head back to the ATL.

It was very cold and windy outside. I could hear the tree limbs brushing against my windows. I was in my bed. My phone ranged. Hello, I answered. What's up, baby girl? Who is this, I asked? It's Jamal from Atlanta. Oh hello, Jamal, how are you? Good and yourself? I'm doing just fine. How's your daughter, Alexis, doing? Alexis is doing fine.

Jamal and I talked about two hours. I told him what went down between Eddie and me and how I got saved and baptized.

I'm sorry to hear about you and Eddie breaking up. You guys were so compatible. Then he turns around and leave you just like that? Yep he sure did, I said. Can't trust no one these days, can you? Just when you think you have it all, all hell breaks loose. Sure does, Jamal responded.

It hurts so bad because I still love Eddie so much. He still loves you too Denise, Jamal said. Oh, I don't know about that. Eddie told me he couldn't stand me, don't like me and don't ever want to see me again. He even told me he hates me. Those are some very harsh words. Besides, usually when Eddie says something so strong, he means it.

Eddie's hurting Denise. Maybe this is his way of showing you he's hurting. Naw. Jamal, Eddie's not hurting because if he was he wouldn't have had another woman laying up with him in his house with him so soon. He would need some time to heal after breaking off the relationship with me so abruptly. Well maybe Eddie needed someone to help ease his pain. To top it off, Eddie married that woman. He definitely did not love me, my friend. Jamal laughed. "What's so funny," I asked? You, he replied. I'm serious though. Denise, if Eddie doesn't love you anymore and doesn't want you, then what's there to get out of his system? That's true. I see your point Jamal.

Listen, Baby Girl, that man still loves you. Trust me. He's hurting inside. The kind of relationship you two had, it's impossible for him not to still love you. That's a confused man who doesn't know what he wants or what he had. He will find out in the end though. What looks good isn't always good. You know that Denise. Yeah, I do. You are so right. Denise, don't worry though. Just be still. Eddie's cookie is definitely going to crumble sooner or later. What he does is hook up with these women and when he gets tired of them, he drops them without warning and moves onto the next woman. You know what Jamal, that makes perfect sense to me. You are so right. Eddie acted like it didn't bother him one bit and that I was supposed to just move on like nothing's never happened. I can't begin to understand him. Right now, the last thing on my mind is another relationship with anyone. I'm still deeply hurt. Enough of this subject, I'm starting to get depressed. I'm saved now. I prayed for him.

So what's up in Atlanta? Nothing but the same old thang. Jamal killed me with his southern accent. Do you have anymore kids yet Jamal? Yeah. I have a little girl name Erika. You need to stop making all these babies. You know southern men, they love making love and making babies. I hear that, I said. Besides, I think my daughter's mom trapped me. Why do men always say that? It's true. I told her I didn't want anymore kids and she said she did so she played her cards right and got exactly what she wanted from me. Well, you should have protected yourself. That's true, Jamal said.

Hey Denise, the reason why I'm calling you is because I'm going to be out of work for about six weeks or until work picks up for me. I thought maybe I could come to visit you up north. Really? God knows I needed the company. Sure, when? I can give you a little taste of the northern side of things. I was thinking of coming up next month. April, I questioned? Yep. That's fine with me. Let me know. I'll call the airlines to make a reservation and get back to you. Ok, cool. Now, I knew Jamal did not have no job that he was going to be out of. Jamal cannot and will not hold down a job. Who does he think he's fooling? All he has to do is say, I'm not doing anything so I am thinking of coming up there. No need to lie to me because I am just a friend. I am not interested in Jamal in any other way than a friendship. He had his time to shine with me and he failed. It was his loss, not mine. But, I would love for him to come up and keep me company. Jamal is a lot of fun and makes me laugh. That's about it. He's not relationship material to me.

Chapter 31

Jamal stepped off the plane looking sharp. He is still a fine brother. Jamal and I have been friends for some years now. We were no longer interested in each other as boyfriend/girlfriend at this point. At least I wasn't. Knowing Jamal, he may have a different agenda. That's typical of him.

Of course when I first met Jamal, we hit it off well. Jamal was someone I could talk to and laugh with. He was cool. We dated for a minute, but it only seemed that we were better off as friends instead. Actually, I had my eyes on someone else. But then, I headed back north.

Jamal looked around for me at the airport. I came up from behind him and whispered into his ear, "looking for me, honey?" Jamal turned around, picked me up, swung me around and gave me a big hug. B-A-B-Y, you looking damn good, he said. Thanks, considering what I've gone through. Hey now, don't start tripping with all of that past shit that happened between you and Eddie. Let that shit go. You're right, you're right, I said.

We went to the baggage claim to get Jamal's luggage then headed to my car. Once Jamal got settled in, he curled up on the sofa while Alexis and I slept in my bed.

The next morning I fixed a big breakfast. I had to cook a country breakfast because that's what southern men like. We had grits, eggs, bacon, cinnamon toast, bisquits, tea and orange juice.

For the day, we stayed in just to catch up with each other. I told Jamal that I was planning on moving back to Atlanta in August. That's great, he said.

Later in the day, I took Jamal down to my mother's to meet her and my sister, Tameka. Alexis wanted to spend the night with my mother anyway.

That evening Jamal and I went to the aquarium and then we went out to dinner. When we got back to my house, we had some wine and listened to slow jams.

Jamal told me the most surprising news. He was interested in me, again! You're crazy, I yelled! Serious, all jokes aside Denise. I know we've always pretty much been friends since you came back, but I still see you Denise as more than a friend. I have always had an attraction for you. You are fine as hell and sexy as hell. You are a beautiful woman and an educated one at that. You sharp too! You have the whole package woman. God damn! Whew, Lord have mercy! I tried to hide it from you, that's all. I tried to be macho, Mr. Cool Man. I didn't know what to say. I just sat there looking at Jamal with a smirk on my face, although what he was saying was the damn truth – every single word of it too. I will own up to that. Maybe he was saying this so we could sleep together. I made up my mind that I'm not sleeping with anyone, especially since I've been saved and baptized. Jamal had another thing coming if this was on his mind. I wouldn't have any problem letting him know this either. All of a sudden I felt uncomfortable in my own house.

Jamal went on and on how I should give him another chance, how he has changed and how I deserved someone who could truly love me, appreciate me and give me things I needed most. I just listened, that's all.

I explained to Jamal how I see him as only a good friend. Jamal is still cool but to me, he is still irresponsible. I am not going back down that road again with Jamal. I am on a different level and my expectations are much higher. The last thing I need is an irresponsible man in my life. I wasn't taking care of a grown man, especially if he couldn't offer me anything if I got down and out. Been there, done that with him. Let's continue to be good friends, I said. After hours of trying to convince me of giving him a chance, Jamal finally agreed with what I was saying to him.

Jamal headed back to Atlanta the following week. He thanked me for everything and the good times I showed him while he was visiting me. I just wanted to be by myself at the moment. I wanted some time for myself. No commitments, no promises, no nothing. I was glad Jamal was understanding of my wishes.

Chapter 32

It was the evening before Alexis and I were heading back to Atlanta. I was packing what little I had left to pack. I left a lot of my stuff in the storage in Atlanta because I knew we were coming back at some point. The phone rung. I looked at the clock and it was 11:00 p.m.

Hello, I answered. Hi, how are you? Good, who's this? It's Eddie. I paused. Oh hi Eddie, how are you? Fine, he said. What is it that you want? Denise, please hear me out. We both acted as nothing had happened between us. I couldn't believe he had the nerve to call me after all this time. The nerve of him.

Eddie told me why he was calling. We talked for an hour about what had happened between us. Basically, we cleared the air. I told him that I was moving the next day to go back to Atlanta. Wow! You always said you wanted to go back. I know. This is the best time of all times. Afterall, I'm laid off from the bank, so I have nothing to lose.

I have to go out to get some gas. Do you mind if I stop by to see you? Why? "Why do you need to see me?" I just want to talk to you and to apologize for the way I acted towards you. I agreed to let him come by. Within twenty minutes Eddie was at my door. He seemed happy to see me, but I was nervous to see him.

We sat down, talked and listened to Teddy Pendergrass' c.d. Eddie talked about him being baptized and his church. I told him about my Christian experience as well.

It got quiet all of a sudden. Eddie looked at me and I looked at him. I knew Eddie had a sip of wine or something. Still the same, I thought to myself.

Remember when I used to suck on your breasts and how hard they used to stay for days? I thought to myself, "is he crazy?" I frowed and was shocked at what he said. What about it, I asked? I was wondering how it would be to do that again. I didn't say anything. I gave Eddie a half of a smile. My heart was racing. Eddie kneeled down in front of me and kissed me on the lips. He pulled my shirt and bra up and began rubbing my breasts, then sucking them. The next thing I knew, we were on the living room floor making love. I don't understand how I could have given in after being away from him for so long. I think I just wanted to be touched by someone. Teddy Pendergrass' c.d. was still playing. I couldn't believe after all these months, here we were in each other's arms and making love to each other again.

You're so beautiful Denise. I can't believe after all this, we still have our chemistry. Well Eddie, maybe this mean something and that something is trying to tell us something. But Eddie, "I can't go back down that road with you again." I'm sorry. I forgave you but you hurt me. You will never know what that feeling was like. What just happened shouldn't have happened. This is all wrong. I think it is time for you to go. I won't be seeing or talking to you again. I have no hard feelings towards you but this is for the best. I prayed to God and ask for His forgiveness on what just happened. I can't go back to this. I must keep it moving.

Eddie told me he still loved me, he thinks about me all the time, he dreams about me and that it's been hard for him. Oh well that's not my problem. He said he would always love me. You're a beautiful woman in mind, body and soul Denise. Always remember that and don't let anyone tell you any different. Be good to yourself. Thanks, I said in a low voice and then rolled my eyes. Eddie is still trying to run that game on me. It's not going to work though. I already know all of this. I have grown so much and my eyes are wide open. I felt the tears rolling down the side of my face. Reality had slapped me in the face because for one, I made a promise that I am not looking back and I had just made the worst mistake I could make with Eddie. That's it, I'm looking ahead because looking back to me is very depressing. I'm done with Michael, Eddie and Jamal for good. I'm history with all three of them. A done deal!

We said our goodbyes and told each other we would pray for one another. Ugh, what a feeling I was feeling.

It's funny how life is. What goes around comes around. I heard through the grapevine that Eddie's wife did him so wrong. Monica deceived Eddie in one of the worst ways by trapping him into having a baby with her. Also Monica's children and Eddie's children did not get along. They were always fighting and carrying on. Monica's daughter did not like Eddie and I heard the feelings were mutual. Just drama. Eddie and Monica finally divorced. I heard it was a nasty divorce too. It all worked out in Monica's favor. Homegirl is getting a large monthly child support payment, she received part of his pension, she received half of the proceeds from the sale of their home which was over forty thousand dollars, Eddie was ordered by the judge to continue paying for Monica's medical and life insurance until their son turns eighteen and to top it off, Monica already had another man she was rolling with and laying up with on the side. And she's living large too. It is so funny how the tables have turned. Eddie did me wrong for this chick and then she turned the tables on him and did him the same way he did me, only she came out with benefits. Again, Monica played her cards right. Monica said she knew what type of man Eddie was. I guess she did. Eddie got played. Monica came from nothing and had nothing to offer Eddie. She used him to her advantage and didn't care whose toes she stepped on or who got hurt. Monica was taking it all the way. She just didn't care. Eddie definitely had met his match this time around. This should be a good lesson learned for Eddie. It's called Karma. You don't want to mess with Karma because when it comes to you, it comes to you three times worse. Eddie needs to remember that "nothing worth having comes easy." Easy come, easy go. Lord have mercy!

Chapter 33

*F*inally arrived in Atlanta. It sure was hot. The movers arrived shortly with my furniture. I missed back east already, but I was ready for Atlanta one more time. That is where my heart is. Therefore, my treasure should be here. Right?

I was so exhausted from the eighteen hour drive from the north to the south. My mother and I took turns driving.

When I heard my phone ringing, I knew it had to be Jamal calling. He was the only one that had the new number so far. I told him I was just arriving and that I'll get back to him soon. Dang, can't he wait! It's not like I'm hooking up with him or anything.

Once I got settled, I started attending Mount Victory Baptist Church. It is a church that definitely got the word across. The choir was awesome! The reverend is a good friend of one of the world's greatest bishops. Oh, it felt so good.

One day I decided to check Jamal out. Only because I was bored that particular day. Jamal is still a liar and is definitely still irresponsible. Of course he hadn't changed a bit. He had no job and to top it off, he lived with his mama this time around. A grown ass man. He makes me sick. Ha, what a joke! Jamal fits the description of a freeloader, someone who is looking for a woman to take care of him and to ride off of what they have so he can kick back, chill and enjoy the ride while it lasts. Sometimes Jamal would stay at his aunt Julie's house and other times he would stay at his aunt Teresa's house. He was from house to house. Househopping. Jamal is definitely not relationship material at all. He's such a waste of my time.

I told Jamal that we would definitely remain friends, nothing more. Jamal seemed agitated with me at this point. I don't care. He is not a man and definitely not my man. Jamal wants to lay up with women and don't do anything. No thank you. He threw up in my face about how women can be and said that he may as well go back to his daughter's mother. Go ahead, I said. It's no shame to my game. I smiled to myself. Do what you have to do, I told him! Because I am doing me now. Life is moving on. Years had passed. I don't have the time nor the engery for any nonsense.

One morning I woke up and decided to continue to stay strong in Christ and to be alone for the moment. Relationships seemed to drain me. I felt good about myself and it felt good to be free.

I had a piece of mind. I was more focused on myself and Alexis. I called Alexis' father, Michael for some money. He sent it. I told Michael that Alexis and I will be out his way for Thanksgiving. He said he couldn't wait to see Alexis. I had no desire of seeing Michael at all. It was for Alexis.

Chapter 34

What a beautiful day the Lord has made. I am taking life one day at a time. Prayer is my answer and my strength. The bible says "do not put your trust in Man, put your trust in the Lord." This is where I went wrong before.

Lord knows I have had my share of putting my trust in a man. It's a known fact to me the men that were in my life have put me through emotional changes and roller coaster rides. Where did I go wrong? Or did I go wrong? Maybe they had a problem and didn't realize it when it came to women. Maybe they were weak men and didn't know how to deal with a real woman.

I definitely have learned from my past relationships. Each one has taught me something different and each time it made me that much more stronger than I already was. I feel I can trust a man and give my heart to a man again. I am making sure that the next time around that I am not going to give the right things to the wrong man. A man has to know his destiny in life, his purpose.

I would like to be with a God fearing man. A man with good spiritual values and who knows the Lord.

142

When I stand before God and witnesses when taking my vows, I want to be ready and be fulfilled by the man that God has chosen for me, not the world. God has to choose for you because he knows what is best for you. This world is so crazy and full of deception. No one cares and no one respects each other anymore. There are so many men that claim the role of being a man or the man, but are not of that makeup. Now don't get me wrong. There are a lot of good men out there. They may be hard to find but they are out there. There's a difference between a man and a boy. A man handles up on his business and knows his direction and his purpose in life, while a boy plays games and has no purpose or no direction in his life at that moment. And us women must have standards and requirements in tact when choosing our mate. If that man truly wants you and knows your self worth, then he will come to terms with your standards and your requirements that you require in order for that a man to be with you. He will treat you with the utmost respect and treat you like a lady, a queen. A man that loves and respects his mother, will love and respect his woman, his wife.

My relationships with Michael, Eddie and Jamal have all failed. I know now why they all failed. As I did some soul searching, I realized that these men were not chosen for me from God. A weak man cannot handle a strong woman with values, morals, and a woman who knows who she is. It is definitely their loss and someone else's gain.

One thing I am certain about is that I am keeping the Lord number one in my life and letting the Lord handle my problems and not to lean or to depend on worldly people for understanding. Also people have a tendency of claiming to help you, get all of your information about your situation and then turn around and talk about you and your situation to others. Again you don't put your trust in Man. You put your trust in God.

It's a crazy world out there. A lot of people do not care these days.

Everyone is all about ME. What can you give me or what can you do for me? It is so sad. It's okay to be there for your man to love him, to support him with his dreams and with his goals, but by all means, make sure that man returns your love, has your back and supports your dreams and your goals as well. "In other words, do not be unequally yoked." The words that I keep close in my heart and in my mind are "peace be still and this too shall pass!" Each time I stumbled, I never fell. Never ever! I am still standing and standing strong through the grace of God. I stand firm and true to what I believe, even if I am standing all alone.

One thing I do know for sure is that "you can't keep a good woman down because she will rise right back up." "Don't hate me, appreciate me." "To love me is to know me."

I refuse to be stuck on stupid. Game over. I rest my case. Peace!

About the Book

Denise – An educated woman who is looking for love but seems to find love in the wrong men. Denise can hold it down for herself. She's sweet and a strong woman. She just simply wants to share her life with someone who can return her love. Unfortunately, in the relationship department Denise meets up with the wrong men who disappoints her, lies and cheats. Shattered and hurt by her past relationships, Denise meditates on why she chooses the men she chooses in her life. Moving forward, Denise comes to terms that the only man who can truly love her is the Man above and decides to turn her life over to Him.

Michael – A banker from New York City. Michael graduated from one of the top universities in New York. Michael meets Denise at the bank. He becomes involved with Denise. Michael seems to be honest and down-to-earth, but his double-life catches up with him when Denise becomes pregnant. Through all of the deceptions and lies surrounding Michael about the so called gang bangers being after him and his undercover marriage to another woman, Denise realizes that she is caught up in a crazy situation and has no direction in which way she should go and confused as to what decision she needs to make surrounding her pregnancy.

Eddie – Was smooth and charming to the ladies. He takes care of the women he becomes involved with. When Eddie meets Denise, he sweeps her off of her feet with his smooth and charming personality. Eddie romances Denise and takes her on a different level she never thought she would dream of. He treats her like a queen. Under all of the smoothness, the charm and the romancing, Eddie shows Denise a different side of him, steals her joy and breaks her down mentally when he abruptly leaves her for another woman and marries her.

Jamal – Is just someone in the passing. Jamal is from Atlanta. Denise meets Jamal one day while taking out the trash. Jamal is cool, calm and collective. He is handsome and sexy. Denise likes his style. They begin dating and a brief relationship forms. When Denise gets laid off from her downtown Atlanta job, she turns to Jamal for support only to realize Jamal offers no support. During Denise's financial crunch, she realizes that Jamal is lazy, lied about working, have no dreams or goals for himself. In fact, the only dreams and goals Jamal have is to live off of each and every woman he meets.

This book is filled with joys, sorrows and pain endured from three different relationships, including mental abuse that started in the early years.

About the Author

Cheryl Bonita Martin was born and raised in Boston, Massachusetts. She graduated from East Boston High School and is a college graduate from Newbury College. She earned a Bachelor of Science degree in business administration with a concentration in human resources management. She lives in the Dallas area with daughter, Sheneé Nicole and her granddaughter, Asia Mikenly. When worshiping, she visits Friendship West Baptist Church in Dallas, Texas.

CPSIA information can be obtained at www.ICGtesting.com
Printed in the USA
LVOW12s1418300314

379541LV00001B/151/P